TOXIC DELUSION

WILD CRIMES MYSTERIES - TWO PREQUEL STORIES

BELINDA POLLARD

For Kate

Welcome to a book by an Australian author! Some of the spelling and punctuation may be unfamiliar but is nevertheless correct. Keep your eyes peeled for uniquely Australian terms.

ARVO. Afternoon. This arvo, tomorrow arvo, arvo tea (afternoon tea).

BILLY, BILLYCAN. A metal cooking pot, with a lid and wire handle, often used over a campfire.

BUSHLAND, THE BUSH. Wild, undeveloped rural areas. Can also refer to wild vegetation.

CARAVAN, VAN. Accommodation on wheels; recreational vehicle without an engine; a travel trailer.

CATTLE GRID. A barrier to livestock that avoids having to open and close a gate. Metal bars are set into a shallow ditch or depression in the ground.

CHOOK. Chicken.

JOURNO. Journalist. Australians love to abbreviate and then add Y or O.

MATE. Friend. Can also be used as an ironic form of address for someone who is *not* a friend.

NAPPY. Baby napkin, diaper.

NEWSREADER. News anchor on television or radio.

OP-SHOP. Charity shop; store where a charity sells used goods to raise funds. Short for opportunity shop.

QUEENSLANDER. The name for a resident of the Australian state of Queensland, but also a distinctive style of house, raised on high stumps to allow cooling air and sometimes floodwaters to pass under its wooden floorboards. Its roof extends over wide verandahs on several sides, providing further passive cooling.

RECCY. Reconnoitre.

REGO, REGO PLATE. Registration number for a motor vehicle.

SCRUB. Bushland, especially when only shrub-height.

SHELL GRIT. Calcium supplement to strengthen the shells of chicken eggs, usually made of seashells or eggshells.

TAIPAN. Highly venomous snake endemic to Australia.

TARP. Tarpaulin.

THONGS. Rubber footwear. (The underwear version is called a G-string in Australia.)

TORCH. Flashlight.

UTE. Utility vehicle. Pick-up truck.

WIDOWMAKER. A type of gum tree or eucalypt, notorious for dropping huge branches without warning.

CALLIE

1

Callie Brown hobbled up-down up-down, dry breath rasping, along a rough dirt track through scraggy bushland, sweaty fingers wrapped convulsively around a worthless four-inch stiletto. Heel, not blade. The most expensive shoes she'd ever owned, destroyed by one jarring step into a hole, perfectly round, made by some kind of natural-born assassin.

She'd snatched up the broken heel because she couldn't afford to leave a trail of breadcrumbs. And it might come in handy…

If this was a movie, she'd have cast off the diamante-encrusted shoes and run, barefoot and lithe, hair streaming. But this wasn't a movie. This was taipan country, where any foot protection was better than none. This was outback Queensland, where her long, frizzy red hair clung like tepid spaghetti to her neck and bare shoulders, forming ever-bigger clumps as she steadily dehydrated.

It was still officially winter for a couple more days, but the late-morning sun roasted her pale shoulders, rapidly tinting them to match the ridiculous magenta taffeta of her tight-skirted ballgown, making her a long narrow bullseye against the monotonous grey-green of the Australian bush.

A glint of sunlight off metal. She peered through looming gum trees and waist-high scrub, swallowing hard against the dust. Cicadas shrieked a demented chorus so loud she could not even hear her own ragged breaths. She licked the dampness from her upper lip, salty and acrid, flicked a quick glance back over her shoulder, and decided.

She hitched up the taffeta to miniskirt height and plunged headlong. There was a structure in there. Shelter. Shade. A hiding place, maybe.

Branches clawed her bare arms and legs. Creepers snared her feet. She lost her balance and fell sideways, smashing her face hard against the smooth white trunk of a ghost gum. She slumped there a moment, gulping lungfuls of sharp-sour eucalyptus scent while not far from her nose a trail of ants, each one as long as a fingernail, marched up to the canopy six storeys above. She rallied and forged on.

The glint turned out to be an old corrugated-iron shed only a little taller than herself and no bigger than a large car. It was being eaten alive by the bush. More rust than metal, closed door hanging askew in its frame. Its roof sagged under the weight of vines and fallen branches. It could have been here, decomposing, for decades, or centuries.

But the padlock was big, and shiny, and brand new.

And that noise? Was that... was that an air-conditioner?

THE EVENING BEFORE

Callie leaned closer to the mirror over the motel basin—who designed the lighting in these places?—and applied one last coat of mascara.

Then she turned towards the full length mirror at her side and took stock. Would it work? The long, strapless dress was silk taffeta with a bit of an eighties vibe and, frankly, a rather bold colour choice. The saleswoman had said, "It's absolutely perfect with your gorgeous hair," and in a weak moment Callie had believed her, and even added to her embattled credit card the extraordinary shoes, so high, so painful, so perfect.

Now, she wasn't so sure.

Magenta satin with strawberry blonde hair had seemed a witty and adventurous combo in a Sydney change room. Now, in outback Queensland after a long day of airports and flight delays, it just looked like the visual equivalent of two cymbals meeting suddenly. Bright purple and orange, basically.

She sighed and wriggled her shoulders. She was probably just tired and flustered. They'd arrived late and then William had hogged the bathroom.

"I'm the host," he'd grumped. "You can come over later."

William Green, newsreader, was presenting the regional journalism awards in the Gemtown Civic Centre. Callie was a television journalist herself, but she could not boast William's level of national fame so tonight she was merely his date.

He'd already sniffed at pretty much everything since they landed: the airport was a tin shed, the town was a dump, and the disorganised and unhelpful woman on reception was… "a Queenslander".

Born and bred in Queensland herself, Callie had narrowed her eyes rather dangerously at that one. But then she'd let it go—because he was tired and because in two months they would be in Italy, viewing extraordinary art and being sung to by gondoliers on canal boats, and William Green would ask her a question to which the answer would easily and naturally be yes. The harder decision would be whether to hyphenate, and if so, should their surname become Brown-Green or Green-Brown?

She shoved her phone into the rather fabulous concealed pocket in one seam of the dress, grabbed her tiny clutch purse and headed across the road, where media personnel from various parts of the state were converging in their best duds. She entered a low-ceilinged room featuring lurid seventies-style carpet full of psychedelic swirls that, unfortunately, almost matched her dress and hair, and nearly fell over at the wall of noise after such a long day. She took a deep breath, drew herself up to her full, magnificent height and scanned the jostle of tuxedos and bling, but couldn't immediately locate William. He stood six-foot-four and she wasn't much less in these shoes, so it shouldn't be quite this hard. Perhaps he was already seated.

The sea of people parted a moment but then surged again, carrying her with it. She grabbed a glass of champagne from a tray sailing past, and then found her shoulder pressed awkwardly against a divider upon which newspaper articles were pinned.

A feature article headline proclaimed CORRUPTION CONTAMINATES COUNCIL CHAMBERS and as she sipped the drink her eyes snagged on the byline: Jack Metcalf. She did a double take, stopped drinking, read it properly.

Jack.

Jack was a finalist. It was a good article.

Was he here for the ceremony? She started scanning the room for a different, somewhat shorter man. It would be so good to see him. To reminisce about schooldays in subtropical Brisbane, and then studying journalism together, their shared love for photography and story and truth and communication.

How had his life turned out? He'd had so much natural skill she'd expected him to be rising to the top in hard news somewhere, creating investigative reports, exposing criminality and cons. But he was obviously still working for the regionals. Doing a good job at it though, if he was up for the major award.

Such a blunt, straightforward, uncomplicated man compared to the moody television star she was in love with. She took another deep breath and her gaze snagged again, this time on the back of a very familiar, artfully tousled dark-blond head above a set of broad shoulders. William.

As she sauntered towards him on those impossible shoes, someone near him moved and she could see what he was looking at: a little blonde with big cleavage in a bright red dress with lips to match, looking up at him with doe eyes.

"William," Callie said warmly as she slid an elegant hand into the crook of his elbow, casting a gracious side-glance at Miss Cleavage.

He turned casually towards her, hands in pockets, fully the superstar, and then his eyebrows crashed together and he said, "What on earth are you wearing?"

2

Callie tore off a sheet of toilet paper and carefully blotted the dampness from under her eyes. William's whole demeanour throughout dinner had proclaimed that he didn't want to be seen with her. Almost every word of the few she had received from him had been barbed. She would overlook it for now; he was tired and cranky. But she wasn't made of stainless steel.

One more calming breath and she left the stall and walked to the basin.

"Excuse me, are you… are you Callie Brown?"

Callie dried her hands and half-turned to a middle-aged woman who seemed to be the only other person in the ladies room. "I am." She reinstalled her professional smile. "Are you up for an award tonight?"

"Oh… no… I'm… I'm not with the media." Callie finally registered that the woman wore the black-and-white of wait staff. "I just… I saw that documentary you made about how, um, even capable women can end up in domestic violence?"

Callie really looked at her then—full eye contact. A

short woman whose neck bobbled as she swallowed hard. Soft-brown, wiry hair, cut into a bob. Kind, intelligent eyes.

Callie's smile was gentle and genuine, this time. "May I ask your name?"

"Shannon. Shannon Cleary."

Callie spoke very quietly. "Are you safe, Shannon? Do you need help?"

Shannon whirled in shock at a harsh double-thump on the outer door of the ladies room. "Why are you taking so long?" a gruff male voice said from outside. The door jolted open and Shannon said, "Nigel!"

A balding man in jeans and a work shirt looked straight at Callie, a smile tightening on his face. "Sorry, miss, my wife isn't feeling well." He stepped forward and grabbed Shannon's arm. "Come on. I'll get you home."

Callie strode back towards the ballroom, senses tingling. What to do? If the man suspected his wife had been reaching out for help, Shannon would be in more danger than normal, tonight. That was the way it worked.

As she entered the ballroom, William's amplified voice, resonant and rich, filled her ears. "And the winner is… Jack Metcalf!"

Applause swelled, and her heart lifted as she looked around the sea of tables. Where was he? Jack would help her do something about Shannon. It would be much easier to confront the woman's husband as part of a pair.

The MC interjected smoothly, "Jack's not able to be here tonight unfortunately, but his colleague Red James will collect the award on his behalf."

William gave that wry, handsome, familiar smile as he handed over the trophy. "No changing the engraving for your own name, now." It was a pretty heavy-handed joke but a titter of laughter went round the room anyway.

Callie began to ease back towards her seat beside William's at the table of honour. He was heading there himself, now, and the MC was urging everyone to the dance floor as music began.

"I need to talk to you," she said as they converged. "Can you come outside a minute?"

The smile on his face was entirely for the benefit of onlookers. "I'm busy. Tell me here."

Was he afraid she was going to start a fight? *Coward.* "I've just met a woman who needs our help. I think she's in danger from her husband. Do you still have duties, or could you come with me?"

He squinted slightly, clashing with the smile he still wore for his public. "What are you on about? Call the cops if you're worried."

"It's not that simple." Not every police officer understood this stuff. And what would she tell them? That she had a hunch?

The eye-roll he delivered definitely didn't match that ever-durable smile. "Nothing's ever simple, with you." And then his gaze shifted to something behind her, and changed in quality.

She turned to find the little blonde, red lips parted, false eyelashes opened adoringly wide. "Would you like to dance, William?" She had one of those breathy, girly voices, like a twelve-year-old in an adult-suit.

William followed the lead of Miss Cleavage in pretending Callie wasn't standing right there. "Love to." He extended a hand and led her towards the dance floor.

Callie turned on a spiky heel and headed for the exit.

CALLIE STRODE to the corner of the building, towards the carpark round the side, hoping that somehow Shannon and Nigel might not have left yet. She stepped straight into a dense cloud of cigarette smoke.

"Hey, Cal! Welcome to cosmopolitan Gemtown." A portly, greying man was making an approximation of jazz hands despite a cigarette in one and a beer glass in the other. It turned out to be a journo she used to work with at a country-town in hot, dusty south-west Queensland, fresh out of uni before she got the break into Sydney.

"George!" She grinned. "How's things?" He started to answer her but it triggered a loose cough that plumbed the deepest sedimentary layers of his lungs. "Still looking after your health, I see."

George sniggered as he tried to get his voice back, and the smoker beside him waved a glass of beer, swayed just slightly, and said, "There's no evidence it causes cancer, you know."

Callie shot the stranger a side glance but addressed George. "Hey, did you see a woman in a waiter's uniform —black trousers, white shirt—come out here with a guy in jeans?"

"Um, yeah." His voice was still a bit rough from the coughing fit. "Yeah, they got in a ute. Already left." As he pointed to an empty parking space with both hands like he was a game-show host, a clump of ash fell from the cigarette and fluttered to the pavement. "Friend of yours?"

"Not yet. Do you know where they live?"

His face contracted as though he was offended. "Nah, mate. I'm not a local."

Callie turned to Mr No Evidence. "Do you know where they live?"

"Nup. Rockhampton." Callie interpreted this succinct

response to mean that he, not Shannon, was from the coastal city several hundred kilometres away.

"Thanks, guys. Have fun." She gave them both a wry smile as they lifted their beer glasses towards her in a mock toast. And then said to George, "Not sure when I'll get back tonight but maybe catch up for a coffee in the morning? I'm flying out at ten."

"Sounds good, kiddo. Take care."

She went back to the street, pulled her phone from the hidden pocket of her dress and opened her ride-sharing app: "not available".

She looked up and down the long, wide street. Shops lined both sides. Their broad awnings extended all the way to the gutter so they could shelter pedestrians from the sun, come morning. Several were boarded up. A fish-and-chip shop seemed to be doing a roaring trade, however, and three friends were laughing raucously outside it as they waited for their order. Further up, a Chinese restaurant spilled coloured light onto the footpath.

In a bare-dirt zone down the centre of the road, between the two bitumen traffic lanes, stood a long row of parked cars—most of them probably attending the event tonight and unable to fit into the civic centre carpark. Owing to spreading shade trees it was gloomy in there, despite the full moon.

Opposite was the motel she was staying in. Maybe a hundred metres away, a blue neon sign proclaimed "police". Hands on hips, Callie tapped her foot and considered going to see them, then decided to ask the somewhat-useless woman at the motel reception, first. It was closer, and less dramatic.

Just as she reached the kerb on that side of the street, she spun towards a taxi that pulled up behind her, disgorging two motel residents.

The front-passenger window was open and Callie leant into it. "Excuse me."

It was the same thin, ungracious, rather weaselly man who'd brought them from the airport, earlier. "Need a ride?" he said in clipped tones.

"Yes please. Do you happen to know Shannon Cleary? Do you know where she lives?"

Silence. His eyes narrowed. "Why do you wanna know?"

"We were having a conversation earlier and got interrupted." She smiled politely. "I just wanted to see if I could catch up with her. Can you help me?"

He stared at her strangely for a long, uncomfortable moment, but she kept smiling, like it was the most natural request in the world. "Get in."

CALLIE SAT in the front seat beside the driver so she could monitor the route. About ten kilometres out of town, he swung abruptly onto a dirt road. She just had time to catch the name Creek Road as their headlights swept across the sign.

The taxi rattled and jolted so much across intense corrugations in the road surface that it was like sitting on an unbalanced washing machine. The driver didn't seem to notice and didn't slow down to protect the suspension; perhaps he wasn't the owner of the vehicle.

Dry grasses, gum trees and spindly shrubs flashed by in the side-glow of the headlights, and she glanced back at a long, wide tail of dust feathering behind them in bright moonlight.

Ahead on their left, a pair of eyes glowed a dull red an instant before the kangaroo startled, leaping into their path. The driver hit the anchors, hard, fishtailing, and Callie shoved her hands reflexively onto the dashboard, jamming her shoulders as the momentum hurled her forward. The man swore lavishly as the roo, taller than the vehicle, bounded past with millimetres to spare. It could so easily have taken out the radiator—or crashed through the windscreen as a tornado of powerful legs and claws.

"Nice save," she said with a dry little laugh.

The driver shot her a glance with the hint of a relieved smile in it this time. Were they bonding at last? He floored the accelerator again, rattling across a cattle grid between two gate posts.

"What do the Clearys do? Farmers?"

The man's shoulders seemed to... tighten? "Miners. Sapphires and stuff."

"Really? How interesting. I suppose that's popular round here. Do they do well?"

The sideways glance was incredulous. "What makes you think they'd tell me?"

"Oh. I guess they wouldn't want to say if they'd struck the mother lode." Did you call it a lode if it was gems? Probably not.

No response.

Ahead, dim lights showed through crowding trees. The driver slowed, crossed another cattle grid, then pulled up before a small, simple, dusty house. The dust cloud following them overtook them, entered the open car windows, and gradually settled on Callie and all the surfaces. She coughed quietly and flapped her hand in front of her face to disperse it.

Dogs barked. At least two. Large and angry, judging by the sound. But they hadn't emerged, so hopefully they were restrained right now.

To the side of the building, three old caravans slumped

in varying stages of decomposition. At the back, light spilled from one of the home's windows, outlining a large shed of corrugated iron with a big sliding door—currently closed and padlocked.

"Thanks," Callie said as she opened the car door. "Wait for me, please. I'll pay you when we get back to town." This was not purely a strategic move to keep the driver onsite. It had suddenly occurred to her that the phone nestling in her hidden pocket, a widely-accepted form of payment in Sydney, might not work out here.

Her gorgeous stilettos were comprehensively unsuited to the rough ground she now walked across to climb three broad wooden stairs. As she crossed a wide timber deck, their heels were just the right size for one to lodge in a gap.

She was just tugging it carefully free, teetering, a hand out sideways for balance, when the front door opened. Nigel Cleary stood there in his jeans, staring. He did not look welcoming. Was that... a splotch of blood on his shirt? Her heart sped up. At least the taxi driver was behind her as backup, sort of.

"Hi," she said brightly. "Is Shannon home?"

"Who's asking?"

"Callie Brown. I'm in town for the awards night. Hoping to catch up with her." She smiled. "You know, a quick cuppa."

He tilted his chin and stared. "How does she know you?"

Damn. Time to bluff. "Cousins."

He narrowed his eyes. "She doesn't have any cousins."

Somewhere in the house behind him, a slightly muffled voice burbled out of a device: *VKR, this is Romeo Alpha Foxtrot, need assistance, over.* Callie recognised what she was hearing even before police communications responded; this man had a radio receiver scanning the emergency frequency, and he had it turned on tonight. Why?

Callie produced an innocent smile. "Well, second cousins. You know what it's like. I haven't seen her in a hundred years." He was shorter than her in those shoes and she slouched a little into a relaxed pose. "Could you let her know I'm here?"

The man reached easily for something at the side of the open door, and it turned out to be the barrel of a rifle. A big, long rifle. He lifted it in one smooth, practised, surprisingly light movement until he had it in a shooting grip, pointing straight at her chest.

The taxi started up noisily, clattered over the cattle grid and revved back down the driveway. And then a cloud of dust enveloped her again.

"Down the stairs," Nigel growled.

Her mind had frozen solid at sight of the weapon, but now it came loose, reeling back and forth: compliance or resistance? Which gave her the best chance? "Where are we going?"

"You wanted to see Shannon." His tone was sour and she had a hunch he was also annoyed with the driver. Plan A had probably been to bully her back into the cab.

Hopefully, the driver would at least call the police before Plan B evolved into something really ugly.

What if Shannon is already dead?

"My partner, William Green the newsreader, will come looking for me if I'm not back in an hour. He's very possessive. And an excellent investigative journalist." She threw a no-nonsense look over her shoulder at him as she stepped back onto the rough ground, the sort of look that said: I'm not a person who can disappear and no one will notice.

But he only rolled his eyes. "Just as well I haven't seen you then. Move!" He jabbed her in the kidneys with the rifle.

She tried to walk calmly and steadily ahead of him into the dark, over pebbles, loose dirt, tangled dry grass. Breathing deeply, thinking so fast the thoughts ricocheted off the walls of her brain, but coming up with nothing. He seemed to be directing her towards the nearest caravan. As her eyes adjusted to the night, she could see it had to be thirty or forty years old, sagging to one side, with a tattered tarp tied haphazardly over the roof by a spider web of frayed nylon ropes.

He pulled a key from his pocket, keeping the gun pointed at her, and opened a door that creaked.

The interior was dark as a cave and a stale, stuffy, sickly odour rushed out at her.

"Inside!"

There was no step, and the van floor was pretty high off the ground for a woman in a narrow ballgown, even in four-inch heels. Unable to come up with an alternative course of action, she hitched up her skirt and lifted one knee high to make the step. She was just raising her other foot from the ground when a large hand planted itself in the middle of her back and shoved.

The door slammed as she fell forward uncontrollably. Unable to get her hands up in time, as the key grated in the lock she face-planted into something… soft? Something that exclaimed, "Ugh!" in shock, or pain, or both.

Sprawling awkwardly, she wriggled free of someone's… stomach? And… legs? "Shannon? Is that you?"

"Yes." It was the merest whisper. "Who are you?"

"Callie Brown."

A soft gasp.

Callie's hand landed in something slimy and sticky on a gritty floor, but she flailed around till she was seated on her backside, legs bent to one side. The stilettos were ridiculously uncomfortable in this position, but she didn't dare risk bare feet in this mess.

Outside, stomping footsteps moved away, then sounded hollow as they ascended the three wooden steps of the house and crossed the verandah. The front door slammed.

What would he do with them now? Did he even know?

She fumbled in her pocket for her phone. It still had plenty of charge, thankfully, but no signal. She turned on its torch function, and let it light them both so Shannon could see Callie's face, too. She looked into frightened eyes, one of which was swollen and beginning to turn purple. The nose looked painful, and a dark surge of blood had spilled down the white shirt and splashed onto the floor.

"Are you injured anywhere else?" Callie murmured.

"Um… my chest hurts, here. And my arm…" She displayed a red and swollen wrist. "He… he usually doesn't hit me…"

"Your legs are okay? Can you walk, do you think?"

"Well, yes… I guess so… but…" Silence.

"We'll have to see what we can do."

"Oh!" Tears glistened in Shannon's eyes in the torchlight, but she was reaching towards Callie's bodice. "Your beautiful dress. It's spoiled." Callie glanced down to see smears of blood across the silk. "I'm so sorry." Shannon's voice roughened and her mouth wobbled. Could she really be that worried about the dress?

"It's absolutely not your fault, Shannon, it's Nigel's. Also, given everything that's going on right now, I don't care much about the dress." She turned off the torch to conserve battery and muttered to herself, "And my boyfriend hates it anyway."

"Probably because it made people look at you instead of him." She spoke quietly and as though it was self-evident. "You looked magnificent in it tonight, especially with that amazing hair."

Callie couldn't think of a reply. After a long pause, she said, "Has he thrown you in here before?"

"Not so much, lately. I've learned not to stir him up."

Callie switched her phone torch on again and rose awkwardly to her feet, taking inventory. One window was large enough to crawl out of, but when she tested it, it wouldn't open.

"He glued it shut. Superglue." Pause. "When I was in here the first time."

Callie stared at her. "The fumes must have been pretty awful."

Shannon just looked down at her hands resting on her knees.

The van must once have had built-in furniture—cupboards, a bed, a dinette—but now it was an empty shell with bolts protruding sharply from floor and walls in various places. There was nothing they could use as a tool or a weapon against either their prison or their captor.

In a far corner, there was a wet patch over some bolt holes in the floor. When Callie realised what it must be, she glanced back at Shannon who looked away, embarrassed. "Good idea," Callie said. "I'll keep that in mind for later."

She found a relatively clear spot on the floor next to the other woman where she could lean back against the outer wall, and turned off the torch again to save battery.

Conversation might help. "So, you do hospitality work, Shannon?"

"Um, that's just a side job for extra money. I'm a schoolteacher, actually."

"Primary, or high?"

"Primary. But, um, I work supply at the moment. You

know… filling in when other teachers are sick? Nigel didn't… he didn't want me to work full-time."

"Oh. Are you caring for your own children?"

"No… I… he… we couldn't have any. And I'm a school chaplain one day a week."

"A chaplain? Like, a religious thing?"

"Well, it's funded by Christian churches, but we're not allowed to proselytise."

"So what *do* you do, then?"

"Help kids going through tough times, mostly."

"I hope you're not going to tell me that Nigel is a Christian." Callie's lips compressed.

"Well… he said he was, at first… but then…" The statement just hung there in the silent dark.

"How long have you been together?"

"Eight years. It's his second marriage." Pause. "My first."

Callie sighed. "Ain't love grand."

"Well it *was*, at first. He was… he was so charming."

"At first." Pause. "Where did you meet?"

"At church." A tiny laugh fluttered in Shannon's throat. "He turned up at my church in Cairns, the church I grew up in, where I went with my family. I was born in Cairns." As though someone had flicked a switch, she became animated, her speech fluent and warm. "My parents ran a fish and chip shop, and we lived behind it in a big, rambling house—an old Queenslander with all these rooms and verandahs added on, over time. We all had after-school jobs in the shop. Five brothers and sisters. Lots of games together, running all round the district after school—water pistols, water bombs. Lots of water!" A genuine laugh. "Mum and Dad saved up all their lives so we could go to university. I went to Brisbane to study teaching, and then I came back, and did my country service in a tiny school about an hour outside Cairns. Commuted every day. Then got a transfer to one of the schools in Cairns a few years later." She sighed. "It was a wonderful life, really."

"And then, Nigel," Callie said.

"Yes."

A long pause. Callie just let it extend.

"We were so in love at first. I couldn't believe it. I was thirty-two, and I'd almost given up on ever meeting anyone. And then Nigel came to town, and he was funny, and handsome, and so good with his hands—he was an auto mechanic. His first wife had been a psycho, treated him badly. He bought me roses and took me to dinner in posh restaurants and everything moved so fast."

Shannon sighed. "And then we got married." Pause. "And then he had some kind of a bust-up with his boss, and lost his job." Pause. "And then he said we should move to Gemtown and make our fortune digging for sapphires." There was a hard edge to that last statement. "And I didn't want to come out here, but I loved him, and I believed in him, so I came."

"And you've been here ever since?"

"Yes."

"Do you see much of your family now?"

"No."

Callie waited again, but the conversation seemed to be over.

———

THE ENDLESS NIGHT EDGED ON, one second at a time. Shannon seemed to have fallen into a restless sleep. Callie listened and waited, uncomfortable, tense and ready, but Nigel didn't come.

Suddenly the door burst open and he was in the room with the rifle, and he was so tall, but… no, it was William. Or Nigel wearing William's face?

She was asleep. She had to be asleep. She fought to wake, to be ready to defend, but she was trapped in a straitjacket of sleep, able to sense the threat approaching but unable to rise through the sleep paralysis.

And then there was a noise. A hiccupping, sobbing type of noise. And then she was awake, and it was so hot in here and she gulped a lungful of stale air, and the bare, gritty floor was so hard under her joints, and beside her, Shannon was sobbing.

Callie tried to speak but her throat was so dry. She tried again, thin and raspy: "What's wrong? Are you okay?"

Shannon shook her head. Her injured arm was red and swollen and she covered her face with her other hand.

Callie could see all this, albeit dimly, without her torch, and tiny slivers of light showed the joints of the caravan and outlined the edges of the door. It must be morning.

And then there were sounds outside. Some kind of banging, like a hammer on wood, but irregular. And… snorting? Crunching footsteps and a key grating in the door.

It opened with a violent creak, and glare spilled in, blinding Callie, but Nigel really did stand there this time. With the rifle. Pointing it at her.

"Up," he barked.

She shot a glance at Shannon, but her head was bowed, looking at the floor, tears streaking the blood that had dried on her face.

Callie staggered upright, wrestling with the tight skirt and one leg that was numb and heavy.

"Out."

She swayed towards the door on the four-inch heels,

and wondered how to make the long step down without losing her balance. More crashing and snorting outside, followed by a gasp from behind her.

"No, Nigel, please! Not the pig!"

Pig? Are they calling me a pig?

"She shouldn't have come," he growled. "She should have minded her own business. So shut up, unless you wanna be out here too."

Callie hitched her skirt and staggered down to the ground, and then she saw it. Tethered to the rear crossbar of a fenced pen only a little bigger than itself, a rope tight around its hind leg. A wild boar, maybe twice the size of a Rottweiler, all curved tusks and coarse hair, with beefy shoulders and tiny little hips—bodybuilder proportions. And very, very angry eyes.

"What are you going to do with that?" Callie managed to keep her voice level but was unable to control her rising eyebrows.

"I'm going to give you a head start." He smiled, his eyes steely and malevolent.

She turned to leap back into the caravan, but he was faster, shoving her aside forcefully so that she was face-down in the dirt, elbows and knees shrieking in pain, even as she heard the caravan key grating in the lock again.

While she scrambled to her feet, breathing hard, he stalked behind the pen and pulled a hypodermic from one pocket. He yanked on the rope anchoring the pig till its hindquarters were hard up against the chain wire of the pen. It thrashed, trying to get at him, but there wasn't enough room for it to turn around. He plunged the needle into its rump.

The pen had a solid gate at the front that raised rather than hinged, like a smaller version of the race they used to contain an angry steer at a rodeo.

The thought exploded in her head: *He's done this before.*

He climbed up onto the fence, grabbing a sturdy tree trunk for balance and, in the other hand, the rope. He manipulated it till the noose loosened, then let it fall off the animal's leg. Whatever he'd injected, it had doubled or tripled the boar's rage. Even in her terror, she found pity for the tormented creature as it grunted and squealed, belting against the gate of the pen again and again.

"I'd run if I were you," Nigel called in a singsong tone. He grinned as he reached for another rope that raised the gate.

Time slowed and Callie's gaze swung like a lighthouse beam. House door: closed, probably locked. Big rear shed: padlocked. Cattle grid front of the house; would the pig's feet get stuck in that, slow it down? It was her only option, so she hitched her skirt up to her thighs and ran.

Seven long, swaying steps in those torturous heels and she was at the cattle grid, then across it. Even over the pounding of her feet and her heart, she heard the unmistakeable metallic screech of the pig gate being lifted behind her.

<hr>

"BAH! GET AWAY!"

From the road, Callie glanced swiftly back over her shoulder at the sound of Nigel's angry voice. The pig was no fool—it knew which person had hurt it, and it was rushing the fence where Nigel balanced precariously, not yet interested in her. The structure shuddered but seemed safe, unfortunately—but it gave her more precious seconds.

Towards the highway. Maybe a passing motorist.

A loud *crack*. Was he shooting at her? Another swift glance—no, he was cracking a stock whip. Down off the fence now and herding the boar away from himself, and towards her.

The rough dirt road to freedom curved as she ran. Spindly trees and scrubby undergrowth began to intervene between her and the house.

How long had it taken last night to get in here? How far was the main road?

She ran on, and more bushland gathered, shielding her from Nigel's view. Suddenly, a rough track off to the side. Two wheel ruts full of potholes—rough, dry grass standing up between them and sometimes overwhelming them.

Breathing hard, she paused an agonising second and then another.

It would be at least a couple of kilometres back to the highway. The terrain between here and there opened out to grassy paddocks. Nowhere to hide in her magenta target-practice dress if he came after her in his ute with that rifle.

She took the side track, plunging into the bushland, going as fast as she dared in these stupid shoes. As a child, playing outdoors with her brothers for endless hours, she could have run barefoot on this track with impunity. But now, her soft city feet would be cut to ribbons, so the stilettos stayed on.

A vehicle engine revved and revved again. The man's laughter drifted across the bush. Was he planning to chase her in the ute or just doing donuts in the front yard?

How did he possibly think he could get away with this? Had he been taking himself the same stuff he'd given the pig?

Has he got away with it before?

She scanned constantly as she ran, looking for anything climbable in case the boar found her before Nigel did. The trees were either spindly and incapable of carrying her weight, or their lowest branches were too high off the ground.

Crashing noises to her right—the direction of the house—and then snorting. Definitely the pig, not the man.

The track veered left. Straight ahead of her stood a large tree, with a strong branch about shoulder height. Did she have the strength to pull herself up?

"If you survive this, you're going to the gym tomorrow, Callie Brown," she panted, reaching the tree just as the pig burst through undergrowth ten metres away. "Or maybe the next day."

She wrapped both arms around the branch and swung one leg in desperation. Miraculously, it hooked over the branch, but the other trailed too low, and the pig arrived too soon, its scimitar-tusk scoring her calf. "Agh!" She suddenly found extra strength to pull the second leg up. Could pigs jump? If it leapt at her, hanging like this, it would have free access to her kidneys and that would be so much worse than the leg wound.

She gripped the rough, sturdy branch like a big purple anaconda, her arms and legs strangling it with all her might. Splinters pierced her skin and deep-red blood dripped from the ragged leg wound onto the pig's hairy back. She swallowed hard and waited for the next injury sure to come, but the pig... seemed disorientated. As though it really didn't know where she'd gone. Directly below her, it swung its head left and right, then shook it up and down, grunting. She clung and quieted her breathing as much as she could. Maybe the drugs were affecting the animal's vision and problem-solving skills, not just its mood.

After about three hundred years unable to find its quarry an arm's length above its head, it trotted back onto the track, paused, looked left and right but thankfully not behind itself, grunted, and moved forward into thick undergrowth, barging a pig-sized tunnel right into and through it.

Callie waited another three hundred years, but it didn't come back. Finally, she released her leg-grip, and then when her feet were firmly on the ground, she loosened her arms—and fell uncontrollably into a trembling silk-satin heap. With a hand fluttering so hard she could hardly move it with any accuracy, she fumbled the phone from her pocket, looked at it… and sighed.

Still no signal.

On wobbly legs, Callie moved again, heading further along the rough track into deep bushland. She had to keep moving.

Her pale skin was roasting in the sun and may well blister before the day was out. Her torn calf pained fiercely and she refused to think about how much bacteria was multiplying in the wound. Her mouth was as dry as the track beneath her.

She jolted and gasped as the suddenly-bare sole of her left foot landed on a sharp rock. Craning her neck, she discovered the missing shoe stuck in the track behind her, its long graceful heel embedded almost full length into a hole in the ground.

She bent to retrieve it then reeled back, staggering, almost falling flat on her back, as sudden movement far too close to her hand resolved into a slender apricot-brown snake about a metre long, camouflaged by the dry grass, elegant head now raised into a sinuous "strike" position.

She struggled to catch her breath. She had nearly

trodden on one of the most deadly snakes in the world. Nigel Cleary being one of the others.

She edged further away, slowly, smoothly, creating some distance, then stood very, very still.

The snake's tongue tasted the air. Eventually, it lowered its head, though still looking at her. She hoped it wasn't settling in for a long nap beside her shoe. Endless moments passed and then it oozled away. Almost immediately, she couldn't see it against the scraggy grass, even though she *knew* where it had gone.

Callie swallowed hard and edged forward again to retrieve the shoe. Still watching the snake zone, she bent carefully to pluck the shoe from the ground, but her hand came up empty. The heel was stuck firmly in the hole.

She gripped the shoe and pulled harder. It still didn't come. She wrenched at it with both hands in desperation. With a *snap* it came away in her hand—minus the heel, which remained lodged in the hole.

She sighed and slipped it onto her foot—the most uncomfortably-shaped ballet flat ever created, the shank that stabilised the shoe now forcing a painful arch and her toes sticking up in the air.

As she turned to continue her escape, a glint pierced her vision. There was just enough of the heel's diamanté encrusted surface still above ground to glitter like a homing beacon in the harsh sun. She couldn't leave it there to help Nigel if he chose to track her. And… the heel was just sharp enough to be possibly useful.

Scouting again to ensure—but unable to reach the desired level of certainty—that the snake was not in fact still close, she retrieved the large, sharp stone that had bitten into her bare foot, and, scanning the grass constantly, used it to dig into the hard ground encasing the stiletto. A few digs, a few wriggles and the heel was free and wrapped firmly in sweaty fingers.

She turned and hobbled up-down up-down as fast as she could, continuing along the track, away from Nigel and hopefully somehow eventually towards help for both herself and Shannon.

Though she'd left the formed road, she was still moving in the vague general direction of Gemtown, and the general direction of the main road. It was the best she could do right now.

She wanted to cry but couldn't afford to waste the moisture. So she just kept running. And running, and running.

4

It was definitely a shed and possibly a hiding place, deep within heavy scrub, almost but not completely invisible from the track she'd been running down for so long. She had to be a couple of kilometres from the house by now.

A glint of metal had alerted her to the structure, but now she couldn't work out why, for this was not a shiny thing.

Corrugated iron walls and roof, bubbling with decades of rust, dripping with vines and forest debris. About the size of a large car and just a little taller than herself.

A huge branch, twice the length of the shed and thicker than a footballer's leg, had obviously fallen from the towering widowmaker gum tree overhead. Its thickest end had speared into the ground on the side nearest Callie. The rest of it lay spreadeagled across a sizeable dent in the roof.

Her hope for shelter was foiled by a large padlock, shiny and new, holding the two sagging doors together. It must have been the steel loop on the padlock that had glinted in the sun.

The shed was… making a noise. A rattling, grinding noise. If she didn't know it to be impossible, she'd have said she was hearing an air conditioner—the old window-box type.

Delirium from fear and exhaustion and dehydration, perhaps?

She tried her broken heel on the padlock at various angles, without success. She shoved the heel back in her pocket and began scouting for a stick strong enough to bash the padlock free. Over the shriek of cicadas, she heard thumping and snorting behind her, loud and close.

She whirled. Shrubbery thrashed. The boar emerged, coming straight at her.

She whirled back and hitched her skirt thigh-high again as she scrambled for the widowmaker branch, grabbing sub-branches, hauling herself up it like a ladder. Spiky twigs and then rust flakes from the shed roof sliced into her skin and her leg wound shrieked anew.

The pig tried to follow her up there, but trotters don't grip tree ladders very well and today was not its day to fly. It butted the big branch, and then again. The shed shimmied uneasily. Would it collapse beneath her?

She crab-walked precariously towards the front of the shed, retrieved the heel from her pocket, and clanged its metal core on the iron door, trying to shift the animal's focus.

And maybe, just maybe, she could use its hostility to her advantage.

The pig paused the ladder attack and shook its head. She clanged again—two sharp taps.

It backed up, and started hunting for the source. She rapped on the door again.

Now it was in front of the shed. Before it could lose interest and wander off, she pocketed the stiletto, leant forward, and waved her arms as low as she dared, right in the animal's line of vision. Right in front of that padlock.

It charged and she scooted back along the roof, her dress snagging on the rough metal, trying to stick to the capline where the roof was strongest, and gasping at the jolt as the boar connected powerfully with the dishevelled doors. It barged and shoved, pulled back, charged again. A deep screech of tortured metal split her ears as the roof joggled.

She had to stop it before the shed fell in a jagged, stabbing heap. Callie cast around for a solution, and grabbed a collection of large twigs with dry leaves attached, and threw them as hard as she could. She was aiming for behind the pig to cause another distraction, but they weren't very aerodynamic and one accidentally landed on its hindquarters.

It rotated, snorting, looking for the next enemy. When would those drugs wear off? Or was it always this determined to get its man?

It looked to left and right, then shook its head and rumbled back into the shrubs.

Callie leaned back on her hands, gulping in air, spreading her weight and trying to balance on the uncertain roof. She finally registered that one hand was on something smooth. Something glassy. She craned to look.

The far side of the ancient shed roof held four gleaming solar panels.

<hr>

CALLIE STOOD AND STARED, open-mouthed, into the dim interior of the shed as tendrils of a sickly, chemical smell curled around her. The pig had not broken the sturdy padlock, but rusted hinges on one side of the door had torn loose. She had managed to wrench the damaged door ajar on that edge, but this would not be a safe haven.

Metal shelves, brand new from a big-box hardware store, lined both sides to the ceiling. They held what must be hundreds or even thousands of packets of cold-and-flu tablets.

A cornucopia of pseudoephedrine. Where did he get it? Had he held up a delivery truck like a twenty-first century bushranger? Or taken advantage of a road accident? A vague memory of a large robbery earlier in the year whispered through her mind.

It was pleasantly cool inside—thanks to an old air-conditioner chuntering away on solar power in an occluded window at the back. Weird. Did he not want the medication to go off? A bench stood at the far end, cluttered with drug-making paraphernalia. Underneath it stood tanks and bottles and boxes. Maybe he didn't want the chemicals to explode in the fierce outback heat.

Nigel Cleary wasn't digging for bling, he was cooking it. Crystal meth.

———

CALLIE FILMED the shed's exterior and interior on her phone, with commentary, and spoke to the camera about what had happened to her in the past fifteen hours, naming names, including details. There was still no signal but she messaged the video to her boss in the Sydney newsroom anyway. That way, if her phone eventually found a signal—whether or not she was still alive at the time—someone would know what had happened out here.

Somewhat miraculously, the shed's equipment included a pair of scissors. Maybe he used them to open the packets. Callie used them to hack off the bottom of her dress to just above the knee, then cut a movement slit each side. Short enough to run more freely, but long enough to still give some sun protection to her upper legs.

A few more snips on the taffeta remnant, a few knots tied, and she had herself a weird little hooded mini-cape that would shade her already-sunburnt face and shoulders.

Next, she gripped her right shoe in both hands and inserted its heel into a hole in a strong side strut of the metal shelving. She tested the movement—one, two, three—and then pulled up, hard. *Snap*. The heel broke off cleanly (clearly a high-quality shoe) and she slipped it into her somewhat crowded side-seam pocket with the other heel and the phone. The collection made a weird bulge on her hip, like she was growing an especially nasty tumour.

She put both shoes on, walked outside and considered her glittering footwear in the dappled sunlight. The section designed to cradle her heel angled slightly backwards. The main part of the foot was reasonably flat on the ground. From the ball of the foot onwards, her toes were forced skywards. They were silver rather than ruby-red, but she pondered how many times she might need to click her heels together to go home.

Home.

Callie sighed as she wrangled the broken door back into place, careful not to touch the padlock or smudge any fingerprints that might be on it.

She stood outside the shed in the shade of the huge gum, facing back the way she had come, as cicadas screamed and her mind roamed. What to do next?

The cicadas took a momentary break and, in the fullness of the sudden silence, behind her came another kind of noise. A long, deep honking sound. Was that… was that an air brake?

She whirled and listened intently but the cicadas

erupted again. If it really had been an air brake, that meant a semi-trailer or heavy vehicle going fast enough to need extra stopping power. The kind of speed that would be impossible on a back road. Could the main road be close?

She certainly couldn't stay here, and now that she knew the dirt track was also used by Nigel, she didn't want to continue along it, either.

She plunged into the deep undergrowth, hoping the pig had gone off to eat Nigel for brunch, and that the local snakes would considerately scatter before her.

"They're more scared of you than you are of them," her father always said—but she doubted it. Intent on making enough noise to shoo them away she almost stomped along in those ridiculous upturned sparkly slippers, searching, hoping against hope for a road.

5

Bruised, scratched and insect-bitten, and with the pain in her calf wound getting stronger and hotter, Callie pushed onwards through bristling undergrowth as she tried to remove the clinging reminder of a particularly unpleasant spider-web encounter. The threads of the web, longer than she was tall, were sticky as super-glue and so strong she couldn't seem to break them. She brushed at them repeatedly until they finally parted company with her arm, only to have them now adhering to her fingers. She tried to wipe them off onto her skirt, but they wouldn't grip the shiny silk and just balled into clumps that still wouldn't leave her hand.

She stepped forward again and, beneath the ground cover, her left Dorothy-slipper was suddenly wet. Water! She pulled the low shrubs apart eagerly. She had stepped into a tiny, grubby little stream. She longed to scoop up a few spoonfuls, but it was just too dirty. She'd be sick for sure, possibly very sick and for a long time, especially with feral pigs inhabiting the area. Just looking at the glistening water made her mouth and throat ten times more arid.

The shade in this denser section of forest was helping, though the air was still hot and dry. She was still sweating; that was a good sign, surely? Her dehydration couldn't have reached the critical point yet.

She cast around for some kind of landmark, something that would help her find this tiny stream again, in case filthy water became better than no water before the day was out. She rotated in place, then pulled out her phone and took a photo of a distinctive fork in a gum tree standing a couple of metres away.

And then she heard it. Behind her. A rumble. She whipped around in time to see a glint of bright sunlight moving fast, horizontally, maybe a hundred metres further, where there was a lightening, a thinning of the trees.

A vehicle. It had to be a vehicle. On a road.

She shoved her phone into her pocket and stumbled onwards.

"Please, God," she said, just in case there was one and He was listening.

A BITUMEN ROAD. Well-made, well-marked. It had to be the main road she'd travelled, leaving Gemtown last night.

Just as she broke free of sharp shrubbery and launched onto the rough gravel verge, arms in the air, waving wildly, a four-wheel drive pulling a long, fancy caravan zipped past at Mach 4, a grey-haired man and woman in the front seats, windows hermetically sealed against the climate, but not sealed enough that she couldn't hear classical music blaring from the sound system.

They hadn't noticed her. The rig disappeared over a rise.

She reassembled the jagged pieces of her broken heart and looked left and right. Which direction would the next vehicle come from? Hopefully not from the Cleary property…

Nothing. Just the scream of cicadas swelling.

A long, straight section of road to the right. That had to be the way to Gemtown, so she began hobbling in the midday sun in her Dorothy-slippers, so very thirsty, hoping.

The road shimmered, heartlessly empty.

And she hobbled. For ten minutes. Fifteen. Twenty-five.

This was stupid. She needed shade or she wouldn't survive. She was about to clamber back into the trees when the road-shimmer at a rise in the distance began to bulge, developed square corners, and resolved into a prime mover—bright yellow. She couldn't really see what it was towing from this angle but it could have two or three trailers behind. He'd need plenty of time to stop.

What if the driver was Nigel's friend or accomplice?

She had to take the risk.

She stepped out into the middle of the lane, took her weird little magenta shade-cape off her head and waved it like a flag, in big sweeping arcs.

Air brakes! What a beautiful sound. The driver wasn't going to just veer onto the other side of the road to avoid her. The truck was actually slowing.

The gleaming cab loomed ever closer, bright bumblebee yellow with a black stripe across the nose. Across the grill a large gold safety sign bore bold black letters: ROAD TRAIN. It pulled to a smooth stop only a metre or two from her, and she read "Daisy-Lee" in elegant cursive script across the top, the dot on the "i" surrounded by petals. Behind the huge windscreen, a round, tanned face beneath well-groomed pepper-and-salt hair looked at her quizzically.

She walked round towards the driver door and the window rolled down. Deliciously refrigerated air fell out of the opening and spilled over her.

The round face leaned out cautiously. "You right, lass?"

"No, mate," she said. "I'm not." She must look ridiculous. And she had to decide fast whether to trust him. And how to convince him. "Are you local?"

He frowned. "No, lass." Hopefully not Nigel's buddy, then.

"May I come up closer?" She indicated the steps leading up the side of the vehicle.

He looked around, back towards the bush near where she had come from. Checked his mirrors. And then back at her. "Righto."

She clambered up and grasped the strong bar supporting the side mirror, but didn't lean too close to the driver's window. He had pulled his sunglasses off and they hung on one of those chains round his neck, slightly tangled with the cord of a second pair which must be reading glasses. He wore a bright-yellow polo shirt with the name "Darren" embroidered across the pocket. "Are you a good person, Darren?" He tilted his head and his forehead furrowed. "It's just that I'm a bit scared. I've just escaped from a kidnapper." She suppressed a rush of unexpected emotion with a deep breath.

His eyes opened wide.

"I must look very wild and strange, but I'm a television journalist from Sydney. In Gemtown for an awards night. My name is Callie Brown."

He nodded, with something that could even have been recognition though she was not particularly well-known in

Queensland. "Well, Callie Brown, come round the other side. You better hop in and we'll get that sorted out."

WHILE DARREN PUT the truck into gear, Callie guzzled from the bottle of cold water he had produced from a small fridge behind his seat. There was a whole Aladdin's cave of stuff back there, including a bed, shelves with paperbacks in them, and a rather self-contained red kelpie named Mud that she had displaced from the passenger seat. The dog, lean and athletic, sat a little stiffly and monitored the intruder—but with side-eye rather than any teeth-baring.

"Do you have a spare shirt, by any chance, Darren? I feel pretty stupid in this getup."

"I do indeed. Let me get off the road. There's a long-enough lay-by about a kilometre further up this way. I'll pull in there and you can tell me all about it and we'll call the police."

As her thirst abated somewhat, she alternated between drinking from the bottle versus holding the cold plastic against different parts of her burning skin.

The spare shirt turned out to be a bright yellow polo shirt with "Darren" embroidered on the pocket. "We can be D1 and D2," she said as she pulled it on over her dress, and he barked a short, deep laugh. It was enormous on her, the short sleeves falling almost to her elbows, so she tied it in a knot at her waist as a fashion statement. "Who's Daisy-Lee, by the way?"

He grinned. "My nana. Now, young lady, tell me what's happened to you."

She told the story as succinctly as she could without omitting any important details, and Darren's face grew more and more grim as it unfolded.

"A wife-beater, a drug dealer *and* cruel to animals." He nodded, firmly. "Let's call the police." He reached for a handset in a cradle on the dash.

"Do you have signal?" she said, surprised, fumbling for her own phone again.

"No, lass. Satellite."

"Oh, great. Oh! Wait."

He had already input 000 but paused with a finger on the "call" button and looked at her, eyebrows raised.

"Nigel has a radio scanner. I heard it last night. If he hears the police putting out the call to a Gemtown unit… he might get away before they can get there." Pause. "Or do something worse to Shannon."

Darren put the handset back in its cradle, sat back, and drummed his fingers lightly on the steering wheel.

It was hard to interpret his reaction. "Do… you think my concern is reasonable?" she said.

He nodded, eyebrows flying up. "I do, lass. But what do we do instead?"

"I'm not sure…" She stared ahead and took a deep breath, followed by a long exhale. "I don't suppose you know where the Clearys live?"

"No, lass, I'm not from round here." He indicated with a thumb towards the empty trailers behind them. "On my way to pick up another load of cattle." Glanced at his watch. "Three hours away."

A memory flashed into her mind. "Creek Road! They live on Creek Road. I saw the sign last night."

Darren keyed his GPS. "Not far. Just a couple of k." He looked at her. "But not a road I can take this rig onto."

"Oh." She slumped. "I hadn't thought of that, but it makes perfect sense." The vehicle was the length of three city buses, at least. It would have a huge turning circle and be hell to reverse.

"Tell you what. I unhitch; leave the trailers here; we take the prime mover. Then, once we're on his actual road we call the cops." A smile. "He's not getting around Daisy-Lee."

"Are you okay with that? Will the trailers be okay? And I don't want to put you in danger…"

He gave her what might be termed "an old-fashioned look" and climbed down out of the cabin.

Callie climbed down herself, fascinated to watch the unhitching process, under close supervision from Mud, who apparently didn't want her getting in the works. Some winding of handles, uncoupling of hoses and connectors, driving the prime mover a metre or so… it was surprisingly quick.

Within minutes, they were turning into Creek Road. Darren pulled to a halt right in the middle of the narrow dirt road, and engaged the brake as the engine continued to rumble. He reached for the satellite phone, and started to dial 000 but Callie said, "Hang on. Can you also do a search on that gizmo? If we can find the direct number for the Gemtown police station, it will save a lot of explanations." 000 would go to a central call centre, probably far, far away.

Darren nodded with a quick thumbs-up, and within a minute, he was entering the direct number with calm deliberation. The explanation was made; the police were on their way.

Darren reached behind, unlocked a long cabinet, and placed a shotgun carefully on the bunk next to Mud.

Callie felt a frisson of fear. What if… what if Darren wasn't safe, after all?

He must have noticed her reaction, even if he misinterpreted her concern. "You're not used to firearms, lass?"

"No. I'm not. They make me uneasy."

"That's a good way to be. They're dangerous. Not toys. But it might come in handy today." He slipped his sunglasses back on. "When we get there, you duck down and hide, and I'll pretend I've taken a wrong turn. Now, let's go and help this poor lady."

IN THE END, Callie didn't have to duck or hide, but she did have to grin. A glorious tableau greeted them as the prime mover rumbled across the final cattle grid.

Cowering on the tray of his ute in the blazing sun: Nigel.

On the ground, repeatedly rushing the ute so that it jolted on its suspension: the wild boar.

Hurling themselves at the walls of their fenced run, furious and vociferous but currently powerless: two huge Rhodesian ridgebacks.

Beneath the door of the caravan she'd been imprisoned in overnight, at least ten metres out of Nigel's reach: his rifle.

Glinting in the lock of the caravan door: the key.

The pig scattered from the rumbling roar of the truck and Nigel collapsed in relief, looking like a man whose rescuers had come; perhaps the sun's reflection on the windscreen had hidden Callie from him.

Darren issued a command to Mud to stay put—"I don't want you getting into it with that pig, my girl"—and stepped down from the cab pointing the shotgun at Nigel.

Whereupon Nigel looked somewhat less relieved.

Callie clambered down in her Dorothy-sparkle-slippers with another two bottles of cold water.

"Water!" Nigel reached for it.

"Wait your turn," she shouted over the noise of the

dogs, and clomped past him to the caravan. "Shannon!" she called as she unlocked it. "Are you okay in there?"

"Callie?" It was more of a croak than a voice, but she was still alive.

Callie brought the sobbing woman out under the shade of a gumtree, enfolded her in a short, fierce hug before letting go—Shannon was red-faced with heat exhaustion—placed one of the cold bottles against the woman's chest like an ice pack, and took the lid off the other one, which Shannon drank thirstily.

"Shut up!" Nigel yelled at the dogs, and they actually did, but whined and panted and paced their enclosure, wild-eyed.

Darren, shotgun still comfortably trained on Nigel, pulled his satellite phone out of his pocket and called the police with an update.

"Oh no," Shannon whimpered. "Not the police. He'll kill me if you call the police."

"No he won't. It's not about you," Callie said. "He's going to jail for a very long time for kidnapping me and manufacturing and trafficking crystal meth."

In the ute tray, Nigel looked sullen. "I don't know what you're talking about."

"No?" Callie tilted her head. "I suppose your fingerprints are not all over the padlock on that shed? Or the thousands of packets of cold tablets."

His face sort of shrivelled, like an old lemon.

"And I suppose the drugs in that hypodermic in your pocket won't match what you've been cooking."

"They're nearly here," Darren announced. "Now, little lady"—he glanced towards Shannon but kept the weapon trained on Nigel—"can you walk? How about you hop up into my cab and have a rest in the cool while we wait. Muddy-girl, hop out of there, the pig's gone now, but don't you go looking for it. Callie, there's muesli bars in there, and some fruit. You get her sorted out, and have some yourself, and I'll keep an eye on this one."

Callie helped Shannon very carefully to her feet. "You're safe now. He's not going to hurt you ever again."

"Good job, lass," Darren said to Callie as he was about to climb back into Daisy-Lee.

"I'm glad you turned out to be a good person," Callie replied around a lump in her throat.

He rumbled off, with Mud sitting tall in the passenger seat, to collect the three trailers and resume their journey to the cattle station, an hour or two late.

Callie was given the front passenger seat in Shannon's ambulance. The sliding door rolled closed behind her, and as they drove off, she looked back over her shoulder at Nigel, handcuffed, being guided into the back of a police cruiser.

Back in Gemtown, Callie received a thorough check and quite a lot of kindness in the emergency room of the small hospital. Cuts and scrapes cleaned, steroid cream for her severe sunburn, a tetanus injection, a course of strong antibiotics for the gash in her calf—accompanied by stern warnings about the bacteria that live on wild boars, and a letter to her GP at home about when to remove the five stitches. She'd have an interesting scar as a souvenir.

A smiling nurse handed her a cup of instant coffee and a sandwich. Callie said, "Ham! How ironic." The nurse looked puzzled, but the doctor chortled.

Nigel should be in a holding cell at the police station by now, if the interview process had finished. Surely, a prison cell would enclose a significant portion of his future.

She went searching and found Shannon's bed in one of the three small wards, awaiting surgery tomorrow on her broken wrist. She lay back limply on plump white pillows, her eyelids drooping as painkillers dripped into her arm.

Callie murmured, "Will you go back to Cairns?"

"Oh… yes. I think so. I just spoke to Mum and she's flying down tomorrow to help me." She smiled mistily. "Thank you so much, Callie. You've got no idea how much it means."

"Alrighty, me darlin' one"—an accented voice entered the room ahead of a tiny, trim, middle-aged nurse. "How about a nice warm shower, and then something to eat?"

A shower. What a beautiful thought.

Callie squeezed Shannon's good hand, then gave her an awkward bed-hug, and moved quietly out of the way.

She stepped out onto the footpath as a four-wheel drive police vehicle pulled up.

"Callie Brown?" A young female police officer was walking round the front of the vehicle.

"Yes, that's me."

"Glad I caught you. We'd like to interview you before you go home tomorrow. Can you drop in at the station in the morning?"

"Yes, of course." *I have plenty to say.*

"Sarge thought we should do it tonight while it's fresh, but I told him you needed a shower and a sleep and tomorrow would be soon enough." She grinned.

Callie laughed weakly. "You deserve a medal." She

stared blankly at her sparkling Dorothy-slippers with their upturned toes, apparently welded to her feet by now. Her brain had turned to sludge.

The police offer was still there. "Hey, I know it's only two blocks, but would you like a lift?"

Callie's gaze swung back onto the woman's face. "Oh, really?"

As she rode the short journey, her phone pinged, and she pulled it out. Her boss. Her video message must have finally uploaded.

> Are you okay? What's going on?

> Yes I'm safe now. More later.

She shoved the phone back in her pocket and sighed.

A couple of minutes later she trudged into Reception. The same woman was behind the counter, playing on her phone. She gave Callie the same vacant look she'd given her yesterday, apparently not even registering her guest's battered appearance. "Yes?" she said, vaguely. Did all her guests arrive this dishevelled, or was the woman just off the planet?

"Is my partner still here?" Callie said.

It wasn't a huge motel with hundreds of guests, but the woman looked like this question was a mystery.

"Room 12?" Callie prompted.

"Oh, have you come for your stuff? We couldn't clean the room…" Rather than seeming either annoyed or apologetic about this, the woman just seemed bemused.

And… William must have left without Callie. Had he been worried? The police hadn't mentioned whether he'd reported her missing and Callie hadn't been able to bring herself to ask.

"I'd like to stay another night if the room is available." It was Sunday night in a small country town. Surely it was available.

"Oh. Oh, alright then. But won't you miss your plane?"

The only plane out of Gemtown left daily at 10.00 am, which this person surely must know, and the sun was now dipping below the horizon.

Callie said, "Um, no. Already missed it, I'm afraid." She didn't have the energy to even begin to discuss it, but thankfully the woman just handed her the key and went back to playing her game on her phone.

The door squeaked open to a room in darkness. Silence echoed. He'd definitely left.

Callie flicked on the light as she shut the door, and caught sight of herself in a long mirror, an apocalyptic vision in an oversized yellow polo shirt with "Darren" on the pocket, a torn and tattered magenta silk skirt, a purple bruise on one cheek where she'd fallen against a tree, and a thick layer of grime and sunburn. Her long hair seemed to have felted together from all the sweat.

At least she didn't have to hear William say, "What on earth are you wearing?" again. Her suitcase lay open on the luggage rack, but his was gone. Her little clutch purse sat on top of her clothes; if he'd managed to bring that back to the motel, why hadn't he wondered where she was? She checked inside; her favourite lipstick was still there, so that was one consolation.

She stepped out of the Dorothy slippers and closed her eyes. Felt her soles expand in relief across the cool tiles. And ached in the centre of her chest. Just ached.

She opened her eyes. "Shower."

She rummaged in the suitcase for pjs. Something red

among her underwear caught her eye. She pulled it out and stared. Definitely not hers.

A lacy push-up bra, in a size to suit Miss Cleavage. And obviously put among Callie's belongings for her to find.

She threw it like a missile into the wastepaper bin and hobbled into the bathroom. Shed her clothing in a heap and set the temperature for lukewarm—she was too sunburnt for hot water.

Minute followed minute as the flood streamed down her battered body, and Callie leaned against the tiled wall and sobbed.

A SHARP WINTER wind whirled off a darkening Sydney Harbour as Callie thanked her driver and stepped from the rideshare vehicle outside William's posh apartment building on the lower north shore. Full-battle makeup camouflaging her bruises and sunburn, just the right amount of wave in her long, glossy auburn hair, little black dress (a Mary Quant lookalike from her vintage op-shop collection), soft-as-butter leather jacket (also an op-shop find), knee-high boots that were pressing a little too firmly on her aching leg wound. She'd prepared herself in record time after arriving home from a long day of travel.

She would have liked to recover from Gemtown a little longer before she faced him—but she had to work tomorrow and needed to see him privately first.

She was about to press the buzzer when a vaguely-familiar resident arrived, and they chattered about the weather all the way up in the lift.

As she reached to knock on William's door she wondered: could the woman have somehow got the bra into her bag without the rest of the activities it implied?

Maybe William had simply been confused or assumed Callie had gone off in a huff, and Miss Cleavage had popped into the room to talk to him or even to return Callie's clutch purse, then waited till his back was turned.

Hope was hard to kill.

The door swung partly open and he stood there in the gap in narrow jeans, a long-sleeved grey t-shirt stretched taut over his six-pack: tall, gorgeous, beloved—even after everything. Frowning. "What are you doing here?" No greeting.

"I thought you'd like to know I'm alright."

"Why wouldn't you be?"

"I was kidnapped." She raised an eyebrow. "Nearly killed by a wild boar, even."

He humphed. "Yeah, right."

"Are you going to invite me in?"

"I don't think so. Callie, surely you can see that it's not working."

The door jolted open an extra distance and a blonde head popped round. Miss Cleavage. All the way from outback Queensland. In his apartment.

Callie's stomach plummeted to the ground floor but she somehow kept a gracious smile pinned in place.

The blonde wore a black silk robe, with little or nothing under it. A robe Callie had worn here before.

The woman's little red mouth opened and her breathy voice said, "Callie Brown! How exciting! Did you know we're going to be working together?"

Working together?

All three of them?

What a treat.

"I'm not sure why you came here without texting first, Callie." William's bearing was aloof and he seemed about to withdraw behind the door. "This is not a convenient time. You know we're not exclusive."

Not exclusive? Since when? "Well, I'm running late anyway, so I'll keep moving," she said, smoothly, graciously. "I just thought you might have been worried when I didn't make it back to the motel." She spun away swiftly before he had a chance to close the door in her face, and concentrated on just staying alive, and breathing, slowly, carefully, as she summoned the lift and tried to hold her soul together.

And I made the mistake of thinking you were a good person.

7

---

*A*bundle of mail in her hand, Callie trudged up three flights of stairs to her tiny, old, rented flat. Everyone assumed television journalists earned huge salaries, but that was only the major newsreaders. Maybe they could have paid her more if they paid William less.

She was exhausted by yet another long day of pretending not to care as he and the little blonde made eyes at each other and giggled over their plans for the Italian holiday he had booked with Callie... while the whole newsroom watched and gossiped.

Never date anyone you work with. Especially if the person they choose to replace you joins the staff too.

The story of her kidnap had created a superb distraction those first few days. Her workmates had especially enjoyed the fact that William Newsreader and the new reporter had been on-the-spot for a great news story but were caught napping. Literally, perhaps.

Although… she guessed they probably hadn't done much napping.

But the news cycle rotated with breathtaking speed, so the kidnap story hadn't sheltered her for long.

Callie had moments when she thought about looking for another job to get out of this mess… but hers was a good job and she'd worked hard to get it. Why should she give it up because William Green was a rat?

She hated herself for loving him. For ever having loved him. For caring what he thought of her. Or that he didn't think of her…

She would ride it out. She would change her focus. She would, somehow, shift newsroom gossip away from their painful love triangle, too.

Inside her little home at last, she tossed the mail onto the kitchen bench between a crusty cereal bowl and last night's freezer-meal packaging. One envelope was thick and textured. A wedding invitation. Who on earth would she take as her "plus one"?

She sighed, tore it open, and stared.

Not a wedding.

Bryan Smithton invites
Callie Brown
to a Ten Year Reunion Trek
through Fiordland National Park, New Zealand
with the Riverside Nine.

And then a list of names from a haunted past. People who had been her whole life, that final year of high school. Including Jack Metcalf, award-winning journalist. She smiled slightly. A good person.

Callie, however, was no athlete and a wilderness trek was a ridiculous idea.

She started to push the invitation aside, but glanced at the dates of the trek, and frowned. Only six weeks away—and matching, almost exactly, the dates she'd planned to go to Italy with William. Dates for which she already had leave approved.

It would definitely shift the narrative. And her own focus, too.

Could she? She ran a finger over the shiny letters, and wondered.

JACK

1

———

The stepping stone beneath Jack Metcalf's feet wriggled, and he lifted his arms, swayed, breathed smoothly, sought his centre of balance and found it. Sometimes, it was a good thing to be not-very-tall.

His mind veered unaccountably to Callie Brown, an old school friend—statuesque with Pre-Raphaelite looks and a scalding sense of humour. She had always seemed to choose towering blokes who looked like underwear models, not ordinary people like Jack. He hooked the thought back sharply and gave it a shake. Why would she be on his mind after all this time? They'd drifted apart since uni and the attraction had never been mutual, which was a mercy, really. He sent up a prayer for her blessing and protection —something he often did when a person dropped into his mind unexpectedly.

The illuminated hands of his divers watch approached midnight. He gauged the distance to the next rock, only half-seen in the gloom, leapt, teetered, but held. They were not planned stepping stones but random slabs that had tumbled into place, probably during a cyclone-fed flood. The river was gentle tonight in what passed for winter in Far North Queensland.

Bare feet would have told him the personality of the rock… but hiking boots were wiser out here, said his dad in his head. His recalled the first time he'd forded this particular river, aged seven. Twenty years ago. Recalled sitting on a rock—maybe even this rock? A hot day, shoes pulled off to allow bare feet to dangle in cool, clear water, sweet juices of a hacked-open baby pineapple stinging a cut on his chin. Siblings ranged on the rocks about him, laughing and teasing, each messily gouging their own half-pineapple with a spoon. Followed by leech bites that took forever to heal because he panicked and pulled them off instead of waiting for Dad to get the salt to sprinkle on it.

He peered down into the gloom; was that a leech snuggling into the top of his sock at this very moment? He'd sort that out later. But snakebite was no laughing matter, so he'd worn the boots. With blister-free woollen socks inside them, despite the humidity of the tropical night. An amazing fibre, wool. His t-shirt was made of it, too— superfine merino, soft and light and stink-resistant.

Moonlight glinted off the river as it rippled past him through dense, uninhabited rainforest all the way to the Coral Sea. From a gap in the treeline on a cliff far above— currently outlined in black against a splatter of stars—the river fell to meet him in stages. Clouds of spray glowed dimly, drifting onto his upturned face in a damp cloak as he closed his eyes and listened.

He was fifteen hundred kilometres from home this weekend because he was supposed to be hiking with a mate from nearby Kulbarton, a small, century-old settlement not that far from the southern edge of the Daintree. Ryan had been a newbie police officer when Jack was fresh out of uni and reporting at the *Kulbarton Chronicle*, both of them on small teams covering big regions. Professional courtesy had expanded into friendship during the search for a lost hiker in this very rainforest.

Two days ago, Jack had slung his rucksack into his ancient hatchback and set off on a twenty-hour drive without air-conditioning, sleeping like a pretzel in a roadside rest area overnight while the ground shook from heavy transports rumbling past a few metres away. He'd walked into the Kulbarton Arms on Friday evening to see Ryan, tall and rangy and grinning a welcome beside his wife, but then raising his arms in an elaborate shrug of frustration.

"You're not gonna believe it. I've gotta work this weekend, mate. Only found out this arvo. The boss has come down with the *mumps*, of all the stupid things."

They'd grumbled together, commiserated, eaten some great steaks, and caught up on what the usual suspects of the district were currently up to, from hippies and fifth-generation farmers to property developers and tourism operators.

And Jack had swallowed his disappointment and adjusted, made it a solo meditation hike. A time to recalibrate before the next term at college began. Refocus on creation and Creator.

Now, it was Saturday night, and he could have been at a noisy awards presentation in a dusty outback town with a bunch of colleagues and strangers made garrulous and extra-cynical by too much alcohol. Had it finished yet, or were they still partying? The organisers had emailed last week to check if he was coming, and he wondered what that meant. Was he a finalist? Maybe. If so, it would be encouraging. He'd entered two pieces: an expose with a stupid headline about corruption in local government; and another one that was a bit of a departure for him, a feature where he'd joined a mountain retreat with others trying to tackle their fear of heights.

Anyway, he'd been glad to have a solid excuse not to go to the awards night.

Glad to be here now, listening to nature, not shouting to be heard over loud music, trying to understand trivial topics and toxic viewpoints.

A nightjar churred. Native frogs trilled. A banging-on-a-hollow-log mating call announced the wretched toxic cane toads introduced by some fool of a scientist generations ago to catch beetles that were affecting sugarcane production. They hadn't even killed the cane beetles—just a lot of precious native wildlife.

And then he heard a koala, wailing like a particularly distressed baby. Unusual, here. Not many gumtrees in the middle of a rainforest—there was no room for them to spread their branches.

So creepy the first time he'd heard that sound—a small boy in a two-man tent in the middle of nowhere with Dad telling ghost stories and chuckling. In a big family, those one-on-one trips with Dad had been magical. Each of them got one trip, once a year. Only now as an adult did he wonder how hard it might have been for Mum at home looking after all the others on her own.

The wailing came again. It seemed to be at ground level, not in the tree canopy. Had the koala fallen?

Two more careful leaps, and he was pushing through crowded undergrowth, parting the spiky fronds of a tree fern, pulling a small rubberised LED torch from one of the zippered pockets of his shorts. He chose it instead of the headlamp on his forehead because he could hood the bright light with his fingers and hopefully avoid alarming the creature.

Cradled in a bowl of mossy tree roots, it was unusually pale. Pink, almost. Hairless.

He stumbled backwards, smacked his head on a low branch. Stared, breathing hard.

It was a human baby, in a cloth nappy, mouth wide, wailing into the empty dark.

2

Jack called, "Hello?" and strained to hear any faint answer that might be drowned out by the frogs and the rushing rapids. He scanned the torch beam around, looking for someone walking, someone resting, or even someone who'd fallen, perhaps. Hopefully not fallen into the river…

No movement. No human voices.

He stooped and scooped up the little body, which jiggled in his arms, a wriggle of arms and legs and angled elbows.

He folded the child in close to his body because he knew babies got cold easily. Thankfully, the night was warm. But what about spray drift? Had the child been chilled? How quickly did hypothermia become dangerous in an infant?

Jack had two nieces and three nephews. The eldest would be starting high school next year, but he'd babysat for pocket money at school and university, and later for free as an uncle-favour, so he knew the basics of baby care. But that was with a list of instructions, a stack of clean nappies, and bottles of milk or formula in the fridge ready to be warmed in the microwave for a strictly-specified span of time.

And even that had made him a little nervous.

It was a whole different category of challenge to be alone in a rainforest with no supplies.

The crying gradually softened. The baby sucked its thumb and nestled close.

He was glad that something—Someone—had woken him, prompted him to experience these beautiful falls by moonlight.

Otherwise he could have made a very different discovery when he hiked through tomorrow morning.

This time, he tried the long, melodious locator-call, rising on the end, well-known in the Australian bush. "Cooee!" This brought no echoing "cooee" in reply—just a burst of irritated tears from the baby.

Jack shouted with maximum volume: "Is anyone there?" More baby-tears, but still no answer.

He jostled his phone from a pocket. No signal, of course.

Should he search further this side of the river, or go back across and retrieve his tent first? He racked his brain for what might be in his supplies that could conceivably feed a newborn. Boiled-and-cooled water would be a start… He had some powdered milk… Was cow's milk safe for an infant? This one seemed quite young.

It was fifteen minutes to the tent, and a full-day's walk from his tent to where he'd parked his car. It wasn't a well-made track, and it would be slow to navigate it at night in dense forest, despite the full moon.

Please, God. What do I do?

Deep breath.

He'd boil some water, pack up his tent and resume the

search. Better to have all his equipment at his disposal as he hunted for the baby's family.

He leapt back across the river, pausing and recalibrating, stone by stone. Adjusting his centre of balance now that he had a little extra weight on his chest and only one arm available to extend.

Who were this family, if they could leave a helpless child to the mercy of the rainforest?

———

THE WATER-FILLED BILLYCAN SWUNG from the back of Jack's fully-laden rucksack, gradually cooling. He'd tried a few different arrangements and finally managed to attach the billy so that it didn't bang painfully against his legs. Once the water in it was cool enough, he'd try mixing some powdered milk into some of it. Maybe. If he couldn't avoid it. If he couldn't find someone with appropriate food before it became necessary.

Well, at least some plain boiled water might stop the baby dehydrating.

Thankfully, he always packed a set of merino thermals wherever he hiked—to the derision of some of his friends. They were small and lightweight and a person could have a fall or some other accident and be in shock and need the warmth, even in the tropics. Knotted around his harness straps, the long johns formed a surprisingly ergonomic sling holding the baby to his chest. Reminded him somewhat of backpacking round Europe in his early twenties: heavy rucksack on the back, day-pack clipped to the front.

A day-pack didn't wriggle and whimper, of course.

Arriving at the bowl in the tree roots where he'd found the child, Jack pulled out his phone and took several photos as a record. He may yet need to take this baby to the police, and he'd need evidence. Then he took off his headlamp and swept it in circles, low to the ground. He was by no means a trained tracker, but he hoped he could find something—some evidence of which direction to search. The track he'd originally planned to follow led deeper into the national park. It seemed unlikely he'd find the family there.

The path wasn't well-marked at the base of the falls, but became somewhat clearer as Jack moved up the hill. He reached a section of nice clear mud, but there were no foot-prints in it. They couldn't have come this way.

He went back down to the river and started a sweep. Eventually, he found a fresh-looking scrape across a mossy rock. Where someone had slipped, maybe? He moved further that way, looking for more, moving out in circles.

While he searched, he processed possible reasons for a baby to be abandoned. Mental illness? Kidnapping? Domestic abuse?

A disturbance in the leaf litter. Beyond it, some useful mud. A shoe print!

The baby made a soft gurgling noise, and Jack felt hopeful. Maybe he'd found the right track.

He kept following, looking for signs, anything. And then he saw something yellow.

It was… a thong. The rubber-footwear kind, not the underwear kind.

A single broken thong, stuck in the mud, the part that went between the toes having pulled right out of the sole. He photographed that, too.

Beyond it in another stretch of mud, a discernible trail, with a bare left foot alternating with a right shoe-print.

THERE WERE two voices—one male, one female. And they were angry. Or scared? Maybe both.

He'd been laboriously following the intermittent tracks for over an hour, constantly turning back and rechecking when the trail disappeared for a few metres. It was nearly 2.00 am.

Jack flicked off his headlamp and listened. They were moving closer, and then they were just the other side of a big clump of tall ferns. He needed to make a decision, fast: if the child was theirs, would he be wise to give it back to them?

"We've got to find him!" That was the woman.

"I know… it's just that—" That was the man.

But the woman cut him off, basically hissing, "How can you still be worried what that man thinks, when he's taken our baby? You should have *forced* him to tell us."

"He's not safe, honey. I mean, we've obviously gotta find Charlie—"

"It must have been *hours* by now." She was sobbing at this point. "He could have been taken by a boa constrictor or *anything*!"

"Um, no, isn't that South America—"

"What! *What* did you say to me? Are you *correcting* me?" She wasn't sobbing anymore.

"—or is it South Africa?"

And she was crying again—loudly. Wailing, in fact. Jack felt reasonably comfortable that the baby could be entrusted to the woman, even if he wasn't so sure about the man.

Charlie stirred, filled his lungs and started howling— and the decision was out of Jack's hands.

3

The woman came crashing straight towards the sound, through the ferns and undergrowth. He flicked his headlamp on to see what was happening but the beam caught her right in the eye and she screamed, hurling herself at him.

"Steady on," Jack said, but she absolutely wasn't listening.

"What are you doing with Charlie?" She grabbed at the infant but he was still strapped to Jack's chest and she was frantically trying to tear him free.

"Wait!" Jack said. "Let me get him untied."

"Untied? You've tied him *up*!" she shrieked as Charlie continued to howl. She kicked Jack's legs with painful force, scrabbled at his face and chest, and the baby wailed even louder. "Give me my son, you monster!"

"Wait!" Jack roared.

And she stopped, then, and stared at him, panting. A young woman, tall and slim, with shoulder-length hair in somewhat of a mess. Even the baby had shut up, but then he started again. A man stumbled through the ferns—short brown hair, about Jack's height and build—and stared, too.

Jack flicked the headlamp beam upwards so that it reflected off the leaves hanging low overhead and gave them some general illumination, but wasn't in anyone eyes. Then he untied the makeshift baby sling with a few quick movements and handed the child to his mother. She clutched him convulsively, her face shoved into the angle of the infant's neck and shoulder. She wept softly and made shushing noises but he kept screaming.

"What were you doing with our son, mate?" the man said over the racket, trying for sinister aggression but speaking a bit too slowly, and staring at Jack with huge, glazed pupils. He was obviously stoned.

"I could ask you the same thing." Jack glared at him.

The father lost his momentum. "What?"

The woman fumbled with her clothing and began to suckle the baby, who stopped crying at last.

Jack continued to address the man. "Why was your son lying helpless on the ground in a rainforest next to a river, all by himself in the middle of the night?"

The man cut his eyes away and the woman spat out: "Next to a *river*?" But she was staring at her partner, not Jack. And then she crooned to Charlie, "It's okay, little love. You're safe. You're all safe." Her eyes flicked up to Jack's but she spoke quietly now. "*Is* he safe? Was he hurt?" Pause. "Did anything bite him?"

Jack spoke quietly too. "He seemed okay. I haven't examined him or anything. I was hoping to find his family before he got too hungry." He quirked his mouth. "I've boiled some water and I've got powdered milk, but I really wasn't sure…"

She smiled at him now, her tear-streaked face luminous. "Thank you for helping him."

He grinned. "I'm just glad I found you before he needed a fresh nappy."

She grinned too.

He extended a hand in the general direction of the warring couple. "Hello. I'm Jack."

The woman freed one hand to shake his. "Astrid." She glanced sideways. "And this useless lump is Elias."

Elias didn't shake hands—he just looked down and shifted his weight, slowly.

Jack shoved his hands into his pockets. "Well, how about you tell me what's going on? Maybe I can help."

ONCE THEY WERE SETTLED, leaning against some rocks and logs, Astrid said, "We came out here for a chicken-pox party."

Jack squinted. "A what?"

"A chicken-pox party." She lifted her chin. "We don't believe in vaccination."

Jack frowned. "Isn't he a bit young to be exposing him to pathogens unnecessarily?"

Astrid grew taller, though still seated on her rock. "We want him to have a robust immune system."

"Oh." Jack crossed his arms and leaned back. Better stand down, for now. Not the main point.

She continued with a tale of twenty-five people gathering for an overnight get-together in an old farmhouse on the edge of the rainforest. Eight of them were unvaccinated children of various ages, one of whom had chicken pox.

"Whose kid was it that had the chicken pox?" Jack asked.

"Max's," said Astrid. "The guy who owned the place."

"His dad's place," her partner mumbled. "Been in the family for generations."

"Oh, yes, you might be right. Or *her* dad, I think." Astrid looked at Jack. "Bianca, Max's partner."

"What was the kid's name?"

"Pardon?" Astrid said.

"Kid with the chicken pox."

"Oh… oh, I'm not sure."

"You saw the rash?"

She frowned. "Um… it was busy. Not very good light under the house. Lots of kids running everywhere. Water fights and so on."

Jack nodded. "And…?"

"Anyway, Eli met this guy, Max, at the produce when he was in town last week." Apparently, Elias was called Eli when he wasn't in trouble.

"You live in Kulbarton?" Jack asked.

"No. We live in Jalunta, on the coast. About an hour away." Astrid shrugged and reconsidered. "Or seventy minutes, perhaps."

Eli piped up. "Buying some shell grit."

"What?" Jack said.

"For the chooks."

"Oh. Of course."

"Some people say you should make it yourself, dry out the shells, but the shells kept breaking anyway, you know?"

"Elias," Astrid said in a warning tone.

"Huh?"

"He doesn't care about the chooks."

"Well…" Jack tipped his head slightly to one side. "I do care about them, but not right now."

"Oh. Right." Eli half-shook his head. "Well, when I said something about Charlie, he asked if we'd like to come to the party, you know?"

As stories went, it was a bit scattered, but Jack had enough of a picture beginning to form. "Was Max buying shell grit?"

"Oh, um… yeah. I think?" Eli looked confused.

Jack continued. "How old were the other children?"

"Various ages," Astrid said. "Three and up, the rest of them."

"Charlie the only baby?"

"Yes."

"Did the others all know each other?" This seemed important though he was still trying to pinpoint why.

Astrid shook her head slowly. "No. Two families travelling round Australia in vans—not together. And others from towns up and down the coast. We all met him in a shop somewhere." She sucked her bottom lip. "I thought it was a bit odd."

Astrid was smart. It *was* odd.

TWENTY MINUTES STRUGGLE THROUGH ROCKS, vines and undergrowth later, they stood together just inside the treeline. They had turned their torches off but in the light of the full moon they could see each other fairly clearly.

Charlie, sated and safe but needing a fresh nappy not currently available, was sound asleep in a cloth sling, held warm against his mother's chest.

Jack was impressed the couple had been able to find their way back to the right place. Eli, despite being off his face and a "useless lump", had used his torch to gouge the bark of trees on the way in.

Jack checked his phone again—still no signal, but the charge was down to about half, so he retrieved his power bank that was about the same size and fitted snugly behind the phone, and joined them together.

A huge house loomed in the moonlight, maybe fifty metres away across long grass. It had a mown yard within a waist-height chainlink fence. A gracious old Queenslander, timber with a corrugated steel roof and wide verandahs on all sides. It was angled on the block so he could see that at the front, two flights of wooden stairs converged into one and climbed to the front door. A very high-set house, maybe as much as three metres off the ground.

Unlike many such houses, no one had added solid walls to the lower storey to create extra rooms. Perhaps the site was flood prone. It was semi-enclosed by the tradi-tional spaced timber palings, with a couple of wider gaps for doorways. Astrid told him that the big open area under the house was concreted, and the house party were sleeping on air mattresses provided by their hosts.

"We wanted to sleep in our car," she said, pointing towards a battered four-wheel drive next to some banana trees. "We can fold down the back seat and make it a nice comfy nook. Flyscreens that fit into the windows. Keep the mozzies out. And another family wanted to sleep in their caravan…" She started to point then paused, frowning. "Um… I can't see it. Eli, where is their caravan?" And to Jack: "Big, glossy thing. Home away from home. Why get away from it all when you can take it all with you—that kind of caravan."

Eli wasn't contributing anything useful, just looking vague and peering this way and that.

"Anyway, Max wouldn't hear of it. Everyone needed to sleep in one space for the party to work, he said."

One space, under Max and Bianca's house. Or Max's father's house. Or possibly Bianca's father's house. Astrid had clarified that both of their hosts just called him Dad.

Whoever Dad might belong to, he was front and centre in this mystery. "They said he has dementia," she said, gaze suddenly locking with Jack's. "When I made a fuss and woke everyone up they said that Dad probably thought the baby had the plague so he'd taken it away from the camp. He's done that before, apparently. And then they said it would be too hard to find them in the dark and he'd come back soon, and it would be too hard to search before daylight." She opened her eyes wide. "Wait till *daylight?* For an *infant?*"

She was angry, and rightly so, but there was another layer to it. "You don't believe them," Jack said. A statement, not a question.

She looked at the house again. "Well... I used to be a nurse. Maybe Lewy body dementia might cause those sorts of hallucinations. But his didn't look quite right, to me." She sucked her bottom lip. "I'm not an expert, of course... but it looked... well, more like he was stoned, really."

Her eyes were back on Jack so he went straight in. "What drugs exactly have you taken?"

She took a step back, arms stiff and straight at her sides, hands curled into fists, eyes ablaze. "I have *not* taken any drugs." Charlie shifted in his sling.

Jack didn't relent. "Something made you sleep through someone picking up your baby, right beside you."

She put her hands on her hips. "When you have personally experienced the utter exhaustion of early motherhood, *then* I'll give you leave to lecture me about what I sleep through." Her nostrils flared.

Jack still didn't stand down, but his next question was softer. "So...?"

She huffed. Then paused. Then looked back towards the house and narrowed her eyes. "The brownies tasted funny. I only had one mouthful and then I stopped." Back to Jack. "Whatever was in it, I didn't want to be feeding it to my child." She flapped a hand. "You know, in my milk." Then a glance at Eli and a little gravel entered her tone. "Elias ate three. He'd have eaten even more if they hadn't run out of them." She wrapped her arms around her sleeping baby and rested her chin lightly on his head, as though it was just the two of them on Earth.

Jack looked at Eli. "Weed?"

He swayed vaguely and said, "Um…"

It was Astrid who gave a useful answer. "I don't think so… A funny flavour… Earthy, perhaps, rather than aromatic."

"So, what do we do?" Jack said.

"I'm not sure about *you*," Astrid said, "but *we* get in our car and drive home. Me driving, obviously." She flicked a disgusted glance in her partner's direction. "Not him."

Jack said, conversationally, "And let them do it again to another family, and maybe succeed this time?"

Astrid's eyes flickered to him and then back to the house. "You think…?"

"A bunch of strangers collected together, most of them far from home, all of them the type of people that don't necessarily play well with legal authorities, all drugged without their consent, one of their babies taken—for someone who wants a baby, I'm guessing, and who was going to retrieve it from beside the river—with an admittedly flimsy story ready in case anyone notices too soon. What do *you* think?"

In the distance, thunder rumbled, though the sky was still clear here. The air was warm and suffocatingly humid.

He saw her neck wobble as she swallowed. She looked at him, then her vehicle, then the house, then her baby.

Then back at Jack. "Well. All right then." She swallowed again. "Let's get in there."

4

———

*J*ack crept along the back of one of the outbuildings behind the house in the pitch dark, running his hand lightly along the corrugations in the steel wall for reference, and listening hard for any movement, anywhere. Quite a large shed, big enough for two cars. The building's shadow carved a deep bite out of the moonlight. Thankfully, the lawn was mown even here and the homeowners seemed surprisingly tidy—none of the piles of detritus often stacked behind such a structure that could trip a person or put a nail through their foot.

Astrid crept along the wall behind him. Once she'd committed herself to not-running-away, she had wanted to ride straight in on her high horse and confront the bad guys with the full force of her righteous rage, but he'd managed to talk her down.

Reccy first. Knowledge and power etc. Anyone happy to drug a bunch of strangers and steal a baby was definitely not safe, as Eli had earlier observed, so they needed to know what they were up against.

Charlie was strapped into his car capsule, wearing a clean nappy. It had been a challenge getting the doors of the creaky old vehicle open quietly. Thankfully, the infant himself was exhausted, relaxed, and well-fed, and hopefully would not be creating any alerts of his own to complicate matters.

Eli was keeping watch from behind the vehicle, with strict instructions from Astrid to save Charlie if things went south. To his credit, he seemed distraught that he couldn't be the one coming with Jack, instead of his partner. Well, as distraught as a stoned person could be. Whatever he'd ingested was acting like rubber shackles on his limbs and his brain and he had struggled unsuccessfully to break free of it.

Jack's rucksack was in the car, too.

He rounded the corner of the shed, still in the moon shadow, and felt the change he'd been hoping for. A door. He reached quietly, carefully. Found the handle. Padlocked, with a sliding bolt. He sighed, very quietly. But no, his exploring fingers stilled, then explored again. The bolt was in place, securing the door closed, but the padlock itself was hanging open, the key protruding from it.

He reached behind, found Astrid's hand, and guided it to the padlock. Heard her sharp intake of breath.

She murmured very softly, "Someone in there?"

He considered. Anyone in there would have been locked in by the bolt, so it seemed unlikely. He drew it back in tiny increments, glancing constantly towards the house. Bright moonlight in the gap should reveal anyone approaching from that direction. In the distance, towards the ocean, storm clouds were piling up, flashing with disjointed lightning.

As he turned the handle slowly it made the slightest grating noise and he paused, stared at the house again. No movement. Hopefully, they were all sound asleep, though he couldn't count on it. Unlikely that the hosts had drugged themselves as well as their guests.

He pulled the door open tentatively, but the hinges seemed well-oiled. He reached back, grabbed Astrid's hand, and pulled her into the shed behind him, closing the door stealthily. There were no windows to let any moonlight in and give them any clue to what was in here, which was both unusual and annoying. Humid, with a musty smell. He hooded his torch and swept it across a surprisingly clean concrete floor, then up a metal table leg to… mushrooms. Thousands of them. Tables and shelves and benches of them. Small mushrooms with a fluted top gleaming dull yellow.

Astrid murmured, "I think we know what was in the brownies."

Jack pulled his phone out and took photos in the torchlight, just a few—close-up and wider shots to give a sense of the scale. This was no home farm for personal use. As he checked one of the pics, he couldn't believe what he saw in the top corner of his phone screen. Still no mobile signal, but it had found wifi. Somewhere nearby—in the house or even in this shed—there was an internet connection, and it was unaccountably unsecured.

His thumbs flew across his screen as he wrote a summary of what was going on, all the names he knew, his best guess at a location, and what they urgently needed, then sent it to Ryan the police officer, followed by one of the mushroom photos, then the photo of the broken rubber thong. He held his breath, then grinned as he saw "delivered".

Ryan would be on-call tonight, but his personal phone might be on Do Not Disturb, so Jack made three wifi calls in quick succession to break through the block.

"Jack! What are you up to at this hour?" It was about three in the morning and Ryan didn't sound sleepy.

"Read the message I just sent you. It's urgent." He tried to keep his voice low.

"I'm in the middle of—"

"Read my message, Ryan! Quickly."

Something moved. Something *inside* the shed. Then a weak voice. "Who is it? Who's there?"

Astrid gasped.

Jack stepped forward, swinging his torch, searching, and stopped on an elderly man with a full head of long grey hair and a scruffy beard, in t-shirt and shorts, lying crumpled on the floor between two tables up the back, straining his neck towards them, holding up a hand to block the blinding light.

"It's Dad!" Astrid exclaimed.

The air pressure in the shed changed as the door swung open behind them.

5

"**W**hat's going on in here?"

Jack swung the torch in the direction of the rough, angry, slightly-slurred voice, skewering a bare-chested, barefoot man in orange yoga pants—middle-aged, a bit flabby, messy hair—who swore and said, "Get that light outa my face." Then, "Astrid! What?" And then, "Dad! How'd you get in here? Where's that baby?"

So this must be Max. Had Jack been into gambling, he would have bet a month's wages that "Dad" was in here precisely because Max put him here.

Before Astrid could jump in with anything that might mess up the plan, Jack said, injecting some tension into his voice, "The baby's not here. Dad doesn't know where he is."

"Ah, noooo." Max rubbed his hair and walked past them to help the old man stand. "Come on, Dad. Let's get you out of here. Where'd you put that baby? Why didn't you come back to the house?"

"Couldn't," he slurred. "Locked. Locked in."

"Don't be silly, Dad," he muttered. "You probably didn't turn the handle the right way."

The elderly man seemed almost in tears and he said it more firmly this time. "Locked."

"Let's get you to bed."

As they went past and out the door, Jack let his torch-light fall down the back of them. Dad seemed fairly clean despite his sojourn on the floor. Max, on the other hand, had dark spots up the back of his orange yoga pants. Mud spots. The kind that flick up the back of your legs when you wear rubber thongs down a muddy trail. His right foot looked reasonably clean on top but the left one was covered in dark mud, including where it had oozed up through his toes.

Astrid gave Jack the side-eye as they walked out into the moonlight behind Max and Dad.

"Does he think I'm Eli?" Jack murmured. Short brown hair. Similar build. Maybe they could get away with it?

She shrugged slightly and quirked her mouth.

"Just go with it?" he asked, and she nodded.

Max stopped abruptly and turned back to them. Dad swayed a little without the steadying hand on his arm. "Better give me that phone."

Astrid inhaled sharply.

Jack shook his head. "What? Why?"

Max extended a hand forward and made a "give me" motion with his fingers. "No photos in the shed. That's the rule." No one moved, except Dad—another little sway. Max's voice dropped an octave and thinned. "Do not cross me."

Jack reached into his pocket and worked his fingers between the phone and the power bank, wriggling till it disconnected.

"Hurry up!" Max growled.

Jack sighed, slouched, and handed over the power bank. Max didn't look at it, just pocketed it, then resumed his passage across the moonlit lawn.

Astrid must have seen, though. Her eyes brightened and her mouth turned up slightly at one corner.

Everyone swung towards the deep rumble of an engine. Car headlights swept across the group and Max froze.

Jack squinted into the glare. Was it a police vehicle? Was it Ryan?

6

It wasn't Ryan. It was a glossy black dual-cab ute, one of the big American ones. Jack couldn't make out the badges or the rego plate thanks to the glare of the headlights.

The engine silenced, the headlights dimmed slightly, the driver's door swung open and a man got out.

Max started walking towards the vehicle, shedding like a cloak his formerly aggressive posture—and also shedding Dad, who staggered.

Astrid darted to the older man and tucked a hand under his bent arm in an ergonomic movement, fully the nurse again. "Let's get you inside," she said quietly. "Get some fluids into you. Wash that stuff out of your system." Then she added, "I believe you that the door was locked."

Dad's head swung round slowly to look at her.

"Things are going to change," she said, and nodded, once.

He rubbed his face and slumped, possibly in relief, and they began slow progress towards the darkened house.

While that was going on, Jack had been easing his

phone out of his pocket, surreptitiously putting the camera on to record video, then folding his arms across his chest, the camera just peeking through the gap between his thumb and first finger.

He ambled out to the side, back towards the rainforest, into the dark, doing his best to look stoned, and rotated apparently aimlessly so his camera could capture the vehicle's number plate and then see the two men converge.

Black-ute man was short and wiry and very contained, in a neat polo shirt and dress shorts, expensive trainers on his feet. Some kind of powerful mood hovered over him— like petrol fumes that might explode if anyone lit a match.

The much taller, broader Max was approaching him for all the world like an abused golden retriever puppy: are you going to stroke me or kick me? "Justin!" Max said, with an ingratiating smile.

"Don't say my name, moron! Where's the package?"

Max reeled back a step. "What?" He looked left and right. "You should have it." Stepped forward and muttered, "Did you go to the right place?"

"Of course I did." Justin inhaled through his teeth then hissed, "These are not people to play games with."

"It was there!"

Justin huffed. "This is what I get for dealing with stoners. Stay off your own damn product. You said yes to this, and now you have to follow through. Whatever it takes." The words dripped menace. "I am *not* taking the fall for you." He angled his head towards the house. "Is there another one?"

Jack heard a car door closing, softly, over in the dark. Thankfully, both combatants seemed too focused on each other to notice.

"The rest are too old. The other one didn't come."

Thunder rolled around, louder, as Justin flung a hand

sideways in a repeated, contained, jabbing movement. "Get rid of them. Out of here. Now."

Max didn't reply, just turned and loped towards the house. As Justin turned slightly to watch him go, the moonlight caught the metallic gleam of something shoved into the back waistband of his shorts.

A pistol.

7

*J*ack slipped behind the shed where his phone could pick up the wifi, rapidly selected a still shot from his video that showed Justin's face and vehicle number plate, and messaged it to Ryan. He added the text in all caps: HE'S GOT A GUN.

He switched his phone to voice recording and slipped it into one of the many pockets on the legs of his hiking shorts, placing it with the microphone at the top of the pocket. Hopefully, voices would still be audible above the rustle of fabric.

The thunderclouds were boiling closer and taller and louder, lit harsh black and white by the moon. Once they arrived, full darkness would come with them. Jack couldn't figure out who would be most disadvantaged or advantaged by that...

As he entered the sleeping area under the house, Max was saying with a jovial air, "Sorry you couldn't sleep in, everyone. Has to be done. Good luck to you all, though."

Sleep in? It was three-thirty in the morning.

All was chaos. Whining children and sluggish-but-annoyed adults. A single bald lightglobe in the centre of the ceiling cast harsh shadows and wasn't powerful enough to illuminate the entire area—it looked like an old incandescent, maybe forty watt. Four or five moths fluttered around it, casting big, looping shadows that must have been even more confusing for those still affected by the mushrooms.

A washing machine stood beside a concrete laundry tub in one corner at the back of the house. Nearby, the door to a small enclosed room stood open, showing part of a toilet pedestal.

Families fumbled in the gloom for their belongings.

Jack found Astrid and crouched beside her, rubbing his face slowly in what he hoped represented a man who'd eaten too many magic brownies, and helped her fold sheets atop an air mattress. She seemed determined to do it neatly and precisely and he could support that goal normally, but maybe not right now. "We need to hurry up," he said through a barely-open mouth, as one family straggled out to their vehicle. "We can't be last to leave."

She shot him a spiky look and muttered, "What about Dad? I think he's the one with all the money. They're using him."

Jack kept looking at the packing. "And we'll do something about it. Later." Should he tell her about the gun? Or would that just make her panic?

As an engine started outside while another family walked out of the sleeping space, he glanced around for Max and located him near the exit to the back stairs, talking to Justin… who was staring straight at Jack, arms crossed.

Jack had a duffel bag full of Eli and Astrid's overnight gear in one hand, a cotton blanket draped over his shoulder, and a travel bassinet in the other hand. Astrid was carrying the baby bag full of clean nappies and all the accompanying clutter.

They joined onto the back of the last family grouping and were heading out into the yard when a firm hand seized his upper arm.

"Not you." It was Justin. "Or you." He grabbed Astrid.

"I think we'd rather just go home for now, if that's okay," Astrid said with a thin smile. Her neck wobbled as she swallowed.

"I don't think so," said Justin. "We'll need to do something about your baby." His eyes were flinty.

Jack really should have told Astrid about the gun…

Justin stepped around them to block the exit, then indicated with an arm towards the back of the house, where Max had now been joined by a tall, thin woman in a floaty, black, kaftan type of thing. Bianca, apparently. She had sharp cheekbones and glossy dark hair cut in one of those asymmetric cuts that looked more Toorak than rural Far North Queensland.

Neither of their hosts appeared relaxed. As Jack and Astrid approached, Max said with an attempt at a gracious smile, "Astrid, Eli." Outside, thunder growled and crashed.

Bianca's sculpted eyebrows drew together in the slightest of frowns as she looked at Jack. It seemed he had finally been discovered to be not-Eli. But she didn't say anything. Just flicked her tongue over the centre of her top lip, shifted her weight, and looked at Max.

Another engine started up outside, and then its noise faded and was gone. Quietness filled the room so full it was hard to breathe, but no one spoke.

Justin sauntered over to the exit from beneath the house, looked around the yard, then sauntered back. Astrid gasped as he pulled out the pistol and pointed it at Jack, arm lifted straight from the shoulder. "Where's the baby?"

Jack swallowed hard and indicated Max. "Why don't you ask him. He reckons his father took Charlie."

"You're not acting like people whose child is still missing." He was absolutely right and Jack should have thought of that; if their search had been unsuccessful they'd have been wanting to call the police, demanding action. Justin kept looking at Jack but swung the gun to point at Astrid's head. "Where's the baby?"

Jack's eyes whipped to Astrid then flickered towards the yard where the couple's four-wheel drive was parked.

Justin gave a smug little smile. "Out." He indicated with the pistol for them to walk ahead of him.

Astrid threw Jack a desperate glance as she moved, but he gave her a look in return that he hoped indicated something like: don't panic.

Bianca said sharply, "What are you going to do with them? This is not what we agreed to."

"Shut up, Bianca," Justin snarled. "It's them or us." He swung back towards her, poking an arrogant finger towards her in time with his words. "If *you'd* done *your* part *properly, none* of this would be happening." He swore lavishly and shook his head. "Such a simple idea. A couple far from home, stoned, who wouldn't be credible witnesses. But you had to make it a *party* and then hide the kid in a *forest*." He shook his head again and muttered, "Stoners!"

As they approached the car, tears were running down Astrid's face.

Justin waved the gun at Jack again. "Open it."

Jack dropped the items he was carrying into a jumble

on the lawn, sent up a quick prayer, and reached to swing the door wide.

Well done, Eli. There was no one inside.

8

Justin swore long and lavishly and with the utmost profanity. He kicked the vehicle. Stormclouds rolled across the sky, quenching the moonlight like closing a blind. Justin grabbed Astrid from behind, hooked one arm round her neck and with the other pushed the gun firmly under her chin, looking at Jack. "Where's the baby?"

Astrid wailed.

Fury on legs burst from behind the banana trees near the car, shouting, "Let her go!"

Justin, eyes wide, turned towards the voice, opening the angle of his left elbow just enough to loosen his grip on Astrid's neck. Jack lunged, converging on him at the same time as Eli.

Arms and legs. A glancing blow to Jack's cheekbone. An elbow to his solar plexus. The feel of smooth metal under his raised wrist and he hooked his hand around it, pushed, flung it away, as they all fell together in a painful, writhing heap. Someone screamed—high-pitched, but probably male.

A blinding spear of light from the heavens. A deafening crack. Lightning! A tree the other side of the clearing erupted into flames and multiple voices squealed in fear as an audible sizzle rolled towards them.

When Jack's vision cleared he cast around for the pistol in the grass, desperate to get to it before Justin or the others.

His eyes stopped at two bare feet, standing astride, then followed them up Bianca's kaftan to find the pistol in her hands, pointing at the pile of tangled people.

———

"Bianca," Max said, a warning note in his voice. "Give me the gun."

"No, Max." She bit out the words. "Enough!" And then, "Get up, the lot of you."

They stood, slowly and painfully. Justin, white-faced, nursed a wrist that didn't seem quite straight. Eli reached for Astrid and pulled her away from the others. They wrapped their arms around each other in a fierce embrace.

"Are you hurt?" she gasped softly.

"I don't know, I don't think so. Are you okay? Please be okay." He ran gentle fingers down the side of her face.

Jack moved off to the other side, rubbing his chest, hunching his shoulders, and trying to get his breath back.

Bianca didn't move the gun. It stayed pointed at the one in the middle of the group: Justin. "All of this stops now." Her voice was a convincing mixture of cyanide and razor blades.

Torrents of rain exploded from the sky and everybody flinched—except Bianca.

The burning tree sizzled some more, and slowly extinguished. The downpour thundered onto the steel roofs so loudly that Jack almost didn't hear a powerful engine approaching.

A vehicle roared through the trees clustered round the driveway, its headlights turning the thousands of huge drops of rain into bright jewels. Spotlights on its roof snapped on, bathing the yard in daylight.

An amplified voice announced: "Police. You are surrounded. Put the weapon down."

9

They weren't surrounded, in fact. Ryan's trick had been a good one for a country cop flying solo into an unpredictable danger zone. It would have given them all a chance if Bianca hadn't been first to the gun. And if she hadn't decided to change sides.

Ten minutes later, they all sat drenched but surprisingly composed in the gracious lounge room of the house as rain continued to pound on the steel roof. Historic family photos adorned the nine-foot tongue-and-groove timber walls. Arranged beneath them stood several antique dressers and sideboards in rich, glowing timbers.

Justin sat on a dining chair, his face grey, his non-broken wrist handcuffed to the leg of a solid, silky-oak dining table, big enough to seat fourteen people, that looked like it had been there for decades or possibly generations and would not be moving any time soon. An ambulance was on its way, along with some police backup.

Astrid and Eli were canoodling, despite the tropical humidity, in a lush leather sofa, dropping soft kisses on each other's faces, one arm around the other and the other two arms working as a perfect team to cradle Charlie, who slept like a cherub. He wasn't even wet, thanks to Eli having had the foresight when he'd taken the baby from the car into the bushes to drape his raincoat—with a gap for ventilation—over the raised handle of the car capsule.

Bianca and Max were sitting as far apart as possible on a beautifully upholstered antique love seat, giving each other filthy looks as Ryan asked them questions and made notes.

Jack sat on another leather sofa chatting with "Dad", who turned out to be the father of Bianca not Max, and whose name was Edward.

"Not Ted," he said. "I don't like Ted. That's a fluffy toy." He was drinking a large glass of milk and emerging just a little from the mushroom fog, making slightly more sense. "It's been a horrible time." His eyes slid towards Jack. "I haven't been well." He scratched his head. "For a long time."

"I think you might start to get better now," Jack replied. "Everything might start to get better, now."

From the snippets Jack was hearing from the direction of the love seat, it seemed like maybe Bianca hadn't been privy to what Max had been feeding his father-in-law. Or at least, how much he'd been feeding him and for how long.

Either way, Jack would be advocating vigorously that Edward be given time and space to detox from his forced mushroom addiction, and find out if he really did have dementia or not. And, hopefully, get back in control of his own life and his own home.

"So, how come you were so close to us?" Jack asked Ryan as they zoomed along the narrow roads. Ryans's police station and home were at least an hour away from the scene.

"Car accident. Big, flashy caravan. Drug driver. One of your fellow party guests, apparently."

"Ah. They must have been the ones who left early."

"Yeah, that sounds right."

"They okay?"

"Yeah. Van's a mess, though." Ryan quirked his mouth. "Stupid thing to be towing on these roads, anyway." He snorted. "Especially if you're high."

"Good thing you had mobile signal."

Ryan grinned. "Accident happened on top of a hill."

Astrid and Eli had been advised not to drive for a few hours yet, and were sleeping off the night's shenanigans in the back of their vehicle, which they'd moved to where shady trees would shield them from the sun's heat as the morning progressed; Eli had pulled out the compass on his phone and calculated the best position, so he must be emerging from the fog at last.

"Do you know what the plan was for the baby?" Jack said.

"One of the big drug families had a customer for a Caucasian baby with brown hair, apparently. I think the parents just work in another country for a year and come back with a new baby and no one's any the wiser."

Jack shook his head. A baby, a human being, a precious family, wasn't for sale.

The first rays of sunlight were glinting off the roof of Jack's ancient hatchback as they pulled into the car park near the trailhead.

"Wanna come back to mine for bacon and eggs and a nap before you start home?"

"Won't you have to work today on all this lot?"

"Yeah, but I can have some brekky first." Ryan grinned. "And you can explain to me how the hell you got caught up in all this drama when you were supposed to be praying in the rainforest or something."

Jack laughed. "And I'll get a notebook out and start interviewing you for the story."

Because it was definitely a story.

10

Jack slogged his way through a college assignment about the relevance of honouring one's father and mother as an adult, and thought about Edward. He'd checked with Ryan, and it sounded like the older man was making progress with his health. Elder-abuse charges had been added to Max's legal burden.

Would Edward be well enough to live alone in his beautiful old rainforest home if Bianca's charges led to imprisonment? Time would tell.

Jack had done the hard-news report on the kidnapping and drug running and sold it to several outlets—including the *Kulbarton Chronicle,* for old times' sake. He'd also put a few things in place so he could follow up later with a feature. It had legs, the bigger story—he could smell it. The mess of drugs and organised crime and family pain and betrayal. Ryan's boss, now recovered from the mumps, was on-side because elder abuse was a hot topic in policing; they'd had an in-service about it a couple of months ago.

Jack leaned back and stared at the painting above his desk: the falls where he'd found Charlie. An unusual mix of acrylic and watercolour. Eli had painted it as a thank-you gift. Astrid had constructed the frame from fallen rainforest timber, which he wasn't sure was legal, but it was done now. She'd carved various motifs into it—including a group of mushrooms and a single rubber thong, revealing an unsuspected sense of humour.

The piece would have pride of place when he had his own home again, but for now he preferred it here where he spent most of his time—above the corkboard in the study room that had been tacked onto the back of his parents' Brisbane house, long ago when they were all in primary school.

Its roof had never been insulated, though Dad had always planned to do it, and the spring sun was unusually fierce today. Shaping up to be a good summer. Heat radiated down from the corrugated iron and flowed like lava over his head and shoulders, seeped into his bloodstream, and pooled under the soles of his bare feet where they connected with the rough concrete.

Under the old wooden desk, Rufus snoozed, his head on Jack's foot. He erupted into an eardrum-piercing bark and crashed past Jack's legs, out into the yard. Jack allowed a moment for his heart to resume normal service, then smiled and stood as the dog darted back into the room with a look that said, "Follow me, this is big!"

"Thank you, Rufus. Yes, it's the postie. The one who came yesterday. And the day before."

He stretched his arms over his head and out sideways as he walked, and relished the feel of grass under his feet. Rufus danced around him, waggling his whole hindquarters. A red-and-white mix of breeds that included quite a lot of cattle dog. Caramel-velvet ears and a thick, brushy tail. He loved it when Jack said his name. To Rufus, Jack was clearly not just some ordinary bloke but Keeper of the Can Opener, Ruler of Worlds.

Jack opened the letterbox and pulled out four or five envelopes. Mostly bills for his parents. Except for one, thick and textured and addressed to Jack.

He propped against the fence, inserted a deft finger under the envelope flap, and shuffled through the documents he found within.

He stared at them, then closed his eyes and let memories wrangle in his head. Days at the beach, trips to the movies, struggling through a group science assignment that no one could agree on and which seemed so incredibly important then, so colossally irrelevant now. Intense moments with Callie in the darkroom—thanks to a teacher who was slightly nuts about film photography—waiting for an image to appear from the beyond, seeping through the shiny paper into the real world, awaiting exactly the right moment to flick the photo into the sour-smelling stop bath so that it couldn't darken any further. Laughter and tomfoolery in Bryan's swimming pool or in front of his big-screen television. Back in the days when Jack still expected great things, before the grind of daily adulthood.

Back in the days before that last evening at Bryan's house…

Jack opened his eyes. His own family home stood solid with its careful gardens and clean weatherboards. He saw the teenager in a sweaty school uniform that he had been, slouching through this very gate with a too-heavy school bag dragging on one shoulder. Being made happy by nothing more astounding than a glass of fruit-cup cordial and a slice of bread and Vegemite.

How far had he come from there, really? Living with Mum and Dad again and thankful for it; saving money so he could do the second degree. Theology. The topic of his heart.

"Waddayareckon, Rufus? Am I a non-event or what?" Rufus wagged and gazed at him, ears flattened. Everyone was more ordinary than they ever thought they'd be. *That's why we have dogs.*

He read the list of names on the invitation. What were their lives like now? Especially Callie, with her fiery curls and irreverent humour. He'd seen her on television sometimes of course, an elegant stranger, and he wondered who she was now that she was so many worlds away from him.

He had been right to let it go. Just a stupid teenage crush, after all, and if she'd ever actually returned the feeling he would never have coped with her disdain for his faith—it was too important to him.

And the name that wasn't there? All of them too young that night to drink alcohol or vote, but forced to shoulder the crushing weight of one obscene, destructive act.

Jack had tried to stay in touch with Bryan afterwards but eventually gave up and focused on his university studies. Prayed for Bryan daily in that earnest, adolescent way, then gradually dropped to weekly, and then not at all. Amazing that Bryan had reached out now with one of his elaborate invitations, almost as if there'd been no long silence. Was it really ten years?

A ten-day hike in the New Zealand wilderness—fully paid for—sounded incredible. The training schedule would ensure he got plenty of exercise during the end-of-term exam pressure. Then there was the mini tough-camera his big family had gifted him last birthday, all throwing into the pot however much they could afford. A documentary in a beautiful national park? Reality style, maybe, as the old friends got to know each other again. Could be fun…

And it might be healing for the group to get together, help them resolve those things that had never yet been laid open to the air.

Yes, those were the reasons excitement was stirring about this invitation. Not Callie Brown and the chance to see her again, all day every day for nearly two weeks. Because that would be a silly reason.

The red dog nudged his foot. He bent to grab the slobbery tennis ball and lobbed it far down the yard, definitely not-thinking about a woman with curly red hair.

Thanks for coming on this adventure with me! Follow Callie and Jack to their somewhat awkward reunion in the majestic Fiordland National Park, New Zealand. In Poison Bay, *when the wilderness is not your only enemy, who do you trust?*

FIND links to your favourite online bookseller at:

https://belindapollard.com/my-recent-books

BELINDA POLLARD

POISON BAY

Wild Crimes Mysteries Book 1
Second revised edition
Paperback: 978-0-6482672-9-4
Also in ebook and Large Print

"The Maori call this place Ata Whenua—Shadow Land."

Television reporter Callie Brown likes safe places with good coffee. But she joins friends from the past on a trek into New Zealand's most brutal wilderness, in the hope of healing a broken heart.

What she doesn't know is that someone wants them all dead.

Lost in every sense of the word, the hikers' primal instincts erupt. Surrounded by people who have harboured secrets for a decade, Callie must choose the right ally if she doesn't want to be the next to die...

———

"Taut suspense and lush descriptions."
LITERARY INKLINGS

"Satisfyingly insightful."
MARGARET NEWMAN

"By turns shocking, satisfying, tragic, and poignant, but ultimately life-affirming."
DEBBIE YOUNG, *Sophie Sayers mysteries*

"So far this is my favourite fiction read of the year."
CLARE O'BEARA, *Goodreads Reviewer*

———

VARUNA FELLOWSHIP WINNER
IPPY SILVER MEDALLIST

VENOM REEF

Wild Crimes Mysteries Book 2
ISBN: 978-0-9945002-0-5
Also in ebook and Large Print

"She surfaced too fast. Spluttering, she trod water gently, trying not to splash, trying not to look like prey."

Television journalist Callie Brown leaps at the chance to make a documentary on an idyllic tropical island—even though she's not sure about working with Jack Metcalf again.

In a remote corner of Australia's Great Barrier Reef, some of the world's most venomous creatures are yielding compounds that could change the face of medical research forever.

When nature turns against the island's inhabitants, is it

a freak occurrence or something more sinister? As danger escalates, Callie and Jack will have to stop fighting each other and start fighting for their lives.

But first, they must work out who among the dwindling group of survivors is determined to destroy them...

"High octane suspense woven with fascinating detail about the glorious Great Barrier Reef—tropical bliss and lethal wonders."
SARAH THORNTON, *Lapse* and *White Throat*

"A fast paced adventure to an island paradise where nothing is as it seems." JESSICA COULSON

"I couldn't ask for a more picturesque location for a story."
DEEANNA WEST

"Venomous creatures, murder and skulduggery ... I couldn't put it down." RUTH COULSON

"What should be seven days on a beautiful tropical island interviewing scientists about their research soon turns into a nailbiting fight for life ... I never knew exactly where the story was going to go, which kept me up reading well past bedtime." IOLA GOULTON

ALSO BY BELINDA POLLARD

AVAILABLE NOW IN EBOOK AND PAPERBACK

FICTION

Toxic Delusion: Wild Crimes Mysteries – Two Prequel Stories

Poison Bay: Wild Crimes Mysteries Book 1

Verschollen in der Poison Bay (German translation)

Venom Reef: Wild Crimes Mysteries Book 2

LIGHT MEMOIR

Dogged Optimism: Lessons in Joy from a Disaster Prone Dog

SPIRITUAL

Meet the Real Jesus: Explore Eyewitness Accounts in 40 Bite-Sized Pieces

WRITING RESOURCES

Use the Power of Feedback to Write a Better Book

ABOUT THE AUTHOR

Belinda Pollard is an award-winning former journalist who loves mountain hiking despite bad knees and a fear of heights. She has been a professional writer and book editor for decades and was a contributor to the *Closer to God* series for many years.

The words "Poison Bay" on a New Zealand map triggered her journey to the sinister end of the bookshelf. Spooky and remote, it was a location just begging for a mystery.

Belinda writes the Wild Crimes mystery series, light memoir, Bible devotionals and resources for writers, and co-hosts the Gracewriters Podcast. Her writing prizes include a Varuna Fellowship.

Belinda lives in subtropical Brisbane, Australia where she wrangles a boisterous terrier and dreams of snow...

To hear news about Belinda Pollard's new books and to receive occasional short stories, go to:

belindapollard.com/subscribe

Connect with Belinda Pollard on social media:

facebook.com/BelindaPollardAuthor
x.com/Belinda_Pollard
instagram.com/belinda_pollard
youtube.com/@Belinda_Pollard
threads.net/@belinda_pollard
linkedin.com/in/belindapollard